The man turned piercing amber eyes in her direction, and her heart skipped. Her breath stopped. He looked directly at her, and she knew what she looked like from there: a dirty, multi-appendaged construction drone, squat with a top mounted binocular camera below a small antenna array; two stubby, multi-jointed legs; and long, flexible arms, each ending in an asymmetrical claw. She wanted to turn and run. She wanted to hide. She couldn't even look away. She couldn't move a muscle, couldn't actuate one servo. They stared, she at him, he at her drone, for what had to have been hours, before, finally, she let out her breath. The drone sagged just slightly, a very organic movement, and the dancer quirked one corner of his mouth into a smile.

Heart racing, breath ragged, Tanni began to take a step back, but changed her mind. She stepped forward instead. As she did, she registered a slight resistance in her forward foot, and the world went black. "What?!" she yelled into the darkness.

Red letters spilled across the blackened world. "Signal lost."

Slowly, she removed the helmet and took one shaking, deep breath. "Oh no…" she said simply and stared ahead at the undecorated wall of her cabin.

RapUnsEl

and Other Stories

CB Droege

Earlier versions of some stories originally appeared in other publications:

"Last Girl" *2013: The Aftermath*. Pill Hill Press. 2010.

"The Admiral" *First Contact Imminent*. Red Skies Press. 2011

"Off Day" *TG Daily*. (serialized)

RapUnsEl

PART ONE - TOWER AND MOUNTAIN

Tanni finished directing EnTa-3, one of her construction drones down on the surface of Venus, and rolled over to EnTa-5, which should have been finishing up with the series of rivets she'd started it on two hours earlier. Inside her controller helmet, she watched from the drone's point-of-view, as the last of the rivets popped into place in a methodical rhythm; three more to go. Tanni used the spare moments to glance at the statuses of the other three drones, each of them doing the jobs she'd directed them in their work zones of the new envi plant.

EnTa-1 had almost finished its walk over to Delta Column, and when it got there, she would have at least an hour of direct manual control ahead of her, as that drone was assigned to assemble a secondary ejector, which was too complex to be automated. She wanted to make sure that the remaining drones were started on automated tasks during that time. Management had been pushing for less drone down-time lately, and she had no desire to be the target of that ire again.

EnTa-5 finished the final rivet and stopped moving. It was always a little disconcerting when a drone finished a task while she had it pulled up as primary. The total stillness was too strong a reminder of their inhumanity. She switched the drone into direct control mode, flexing its appendages and using the camera to look around in a way she thought of as organic. She shrugged and saw the drone's view bob, as it matched the movement. Taking direct control was slipping into a distant skin. The sheer immersion surprised her every time. Reflexively, she turned to look up toward the city station, where she knew her body was sitting, tied into the control helmet. It was impossible to see Venusberg (Venus Station One, but no one ever called it that) from the surface, of course. The sky was only a mass of thick blue-green clouds over the twisted grey landscape of the mostly dead planet, and besides, the station was nearly fifty kilometers away.

This envi plant would be the next step in terraforming Venus. In a few years, this facility would start converting carbon dioxide into oxygen, doing the work of a thousand forests. Many decades later, the structures would dot the surface of the planet, and in those days, the domes would come down, and the homesteaders would begin to arrive, the way they already had on Mars, where they claimed bare craters and canals and converted them into new settlements back when Venus was just starting to get its upper atmosphere scrubbed of sulfuric acid by the first aerostat installations, which were still working slowly, somewhere in the atmosphere between Tanni and her drones.

"Controller Tannhauser." The voice broke her reverie, and she squealed in surprise. Emily Urban's soft face appeared on a small panel in her peripheral vision.

"Emily!" Tanni caught her breath. "You nearly made me jump right off the top of Beta Column."

"Sorry, Tanni," the woman replied, her face frowning. "Our scope on your feed is still wonk. I didn't know you were in D.C. mode. I'll knock first next time."

"It's okay…" Tanni took a deep breath to settle her jumpstarted nerves. "What is it?"

"I just thought you'd want to know, *RapUnsEl* is nearly at base station."

Without thinking, Tanni turned to look at the skyhook, seeing it as a thin black line running from the distant central complex up into the blue-grey clouds. As she watched, the *RapUnsEl* broke through those clouds, looking like a majestic barge falling out of the sky, which, she supposed, was pretty close to what it was. At this distance, it didn't look rapid, unsheltered, or very much like an elevator, but she knew that it was moving at several hundred kilometers per hour, despite appearances, and while it was enclosed, it was not airtight, except for the single small passenger cabin. Of course, whether or not it was an "elevator" was a topic of debate in the galley at least once a week. Tanni tried not to take sides.

"At last," Tanni said. "I've been short a drone for a month." The *RapUnsEl* took 12 days to make a round trip, so any supplies were always long in arriving.

"I'm switching EnTa-7 on now," Emily said. "It should be within range of the control tower."

"Thanks, Commander." Emily's title was "Lead Controller," but that didn't roll off the tongue as well.

"Just don't lose this one." Emily smiled wryly before signing off, her face disappearing from view.

In a few moments, Tanni saw a new feed appear in her control panel. She directed EnTa-5 to descend the column on its own, and she rolled over to the new drone. EnTa-7 was a newer model than her other units, had better articulated limbs, and was supposed to be a more natural control process. The view she was presented with was a bare grey panel, the drone must be pressed up against a wall. She shrugged into direct control, and the drone's weight shifted back, taking her off balance. She felt like she was falling for a moment before the drone's gyros kicked in to stabilize her.

"Well, you'll need some breaking in," she said aloud. Then she heard her own voice bounce back to her from the drone's mic. She had forgotten that this new model also had a speaker, tied into the mic in her control helmet. She quickly switched the speaker off and was glad that there could not have been anyone around to hear her drone talking to itself.

She tried to back away from the wall, but she was pinned. Turning to look around, she saw other cargo, mostly building materials and supplies for the residents in the buildings on the surface. She managed to climb the drone onto a crate of bullion (one of the few food products that was easier to import from Earth than make on Venus) along the wall to escape. There were no windows in the *RapUnsEl*, but there were some slits in the walls and ceiling to make sure that pressure was always equalized. She stepped over to one of these slits and looked out. From here she could see the incomplete envi plant. She looked at Beta Column and smiled to see EnTa-5 slowly climbing down the edge of the structure. It passed within a few feet of another drone; her HUD told her it was EnSm-4. That was one of Smitty's drones. He was twenty meters away from her up in Venusberg, but they rarely spoke. The drones, of course, did not acknowledge each other.

She couldn't see the base station itself from here, as it was directly below her, but this was likely a good thing, as seeing the rapidly approaching landing site for the *RapUnsEl* would likely give her vertigo, especially from the vantage of a drone she was unused to. She could, however, see the sprawling complex connected to it. The closest were the habitation towers, looking like miniature versions of the arcologies back on Earth: spindly, twisting towers with lots of glass for greenhouses. People mostly lived toward the center of each tower, while food was grown along the sides.

Beyond the towers, a series of domes and cubes connected by tunnels and skywalks spread for several miles. Many of these were research stations, but some were for additional farming, and still fewer were early attempts at manufacturing to cut down on what tools and supplies needed to come from Earth. It wasn't working well yet. The only products they could make were the ones for which production could be fully automated. There simply weren't many manual laborers in the Venus compound. Everyone came here to work in construction, like Tanni and her fellow Controllers, or pure science. Perhaps in a couple generations there would be some young people who would want to work on assembly lines, but she doubted it. That kind of work would always be left to the Earth.

Tanni didn't get to see this view often, so she remained and continued to watch as the *RapUnsEl* decelerated during the final half-mile of its five-day decent. In a few minutes, the vehicle touched down on the roof of the base station, settling into a cradle that conformed perfectly to the bottom of the carriage. The main gates opened on one side, and Tanni climbed her drone carefully down off of the crate of bullion and navigated her way off of the platform.

She was anxious to run the new drone through its paces, but that would have to wait. EnTa-1 was already signaling her - with infinite patience - that it was ready for its manual task. She started EnTa-7 toward the towers of the envi plant in the distance, and then she rolled over to EnTa-1.

She was staring at a jumbled pile of unlabeled parts that needed to become a secondary ejector.

Tanni's sleep shift was approaching when she got the warning that EnTa-7 was outside the work area. *Of course it is*, she thought, *it's only been two hours, it's still on its way to the work area.*

She had finished the secondary ejector fifteen minutes ago and was simply watching EnTa-4 paint an interior corridor. It was the most interesting job any of her drones was working on at the time. She pulled up EnTa-7's camera feed to see how far it had gotten, expecting it to be somewhere around the outer arcology ring by now. Probably another few minutes before she would need to give it explicit destination instructions.

The view she saw from EnTa-7, however, was not what she expected. In place of the twisted arcology bases, skywalks, and research cubes, she saw only bare Venusian plains. She rolled her view over to the new drone and took manual control of the camera, turning it 180 degrees to look back at the four spires of the new envi plant. "Oops!" she said aloud. "I guess you're a bit faster than the others too!"

Tanni switched the drone into full control mode and felt the mild vertigo again as she shrugged into the still unfamiliar dimensions of EnTa-7. She slowed the forward progress of the drone to a stop, then began turning the camera back around as the wheels retracted and the legs folded back into place. That's when she saw the dancer.

She was looking at one of the most distant research complexes, the one leased to Türme Industries, if she was remembering it right: the biotech division, or maybe they were bioengineering? Was there a difference? She couldn't remember, and she wasn't thinking about it very closely anyway. She was distracted. One of the outermost nodes of this outer complex was a geodesic glass dome. She hadn't been part of the team that built that node, but she'd seen it before, glittering like a many-faceted jewel in the distance when a rare break in the clouds managed to bring in a blast of full sunlight on the base. Many places on the surface would glitter when this happened but none of them quite like this crystal dome. On sunny days, she would seek it out to watch it sparkle, but presently it was not the glass that held her attention — it was someone inside.

Among the dense foliage, broad-leafed plants, and fruit trees that nearly filled the ground inside the dome to capacity, a lone figure, silhouetted against the greenery, was dancing. A male form in skin-tight clothes was leaping, spinning, and pointing. Tanni didn't know much about dance, but she knew ballet when she saw it. He was beautiful. In form and athleticism, he was surely skilled, though she wouldn't honestly know, but she knew he was beautiful.

Involuntarily, she took a step toward his covered stage, then another, and another. When she realized what she was doing, she stopped, and shook her head as if to clear the daze from it. She felt intense vertigo as the drone whipped it's camera from side to side in response. She stumbled forward, and the drone's internal gyros saved her from toppling for a second time since its activation. Miles above, in Venusberg, she fell out of the chair her body was resting in, and the control helmet shut off.

She was lying on the floor. She pulled off the helmet, her kinky, damp hair falling into her face. She was sweating, and her breath was coming heavy. She hadn't had such a terrible time with drone control since she was a student. What was so difficult with this one?

She pulled herself up and dusted herself off. She felt like a mess. She needed sleep, and she needed a shower. She sat back in the chair, reconnected the data-feed to the helmet, and replaced the helmet on her head, going immediately back into direct control mode for EnTa-7.

When she reoriented herself, and looked back to the dome, she couldn't find the dancer among the trees. Had he spotted her? Was he hiding? She felt bad then. She was a voyeur, a peeper. She'd made an innocent, beautiful man feel spied upon.

She was about to turn away, to turn back to her work and forget having ever seen him, when he reemerged. He stepped out of a corner, past a pair of modified apple trees on this side of the small garden, a mere ten yards away. He held a towel in one hand and a bottle in the other. He sprayed water from the bottle into his open mouth, then over his dark face, and into his hair, letting it drip down his leotard where it mingled with his sweat. She could see his face now, heart-shaped with high cheekbones and a cleft chin. Long, wavy hair tumbled over his shoulders. Tanni felt her face flush. She licked her lips and shifted her body a bit in her chair to relieve a certain antsyness. The drone responded and wiggled in place just slightly.

The man turned piercing amber eyes in her direction, and her heart skipped. Her breath stopped. He looked directly at her, and she knew what she looked like from there: a dirty, multi-appendaged construction drone, squat with a top mounted binocular camera below a small antenna array; two stubby, multi-jointed legs; and long, flexible arms, each ending in an asymmetrical claw. She wanted to turn and run. She wanted to hide. She couldn't even look away. She couldn't move a muscle, couldn't actuate one servo. They stared, she at him, he at her drone, for what had to have been hours, before, finally, she let out her breath. The drone sagged just slightly, a very organic movement, and the dancer quirked one corner of his mouth into a smile.

Heart racing, breath ragged, Tanni began to take a step back, but changed her mind. She stepped forward instead. As she did, she registered a slight resistance in her forward foot, and the world went black. "What?!" she yelled into the darkness.

Red letters spilled across the blackened world. "Signal lost."

Slowly, she removed the helmet and took one shaking, deep breath. "Oh no…" she said simply and stared ahead at the undecorated wall of her cabin.

"It was too fast?!" Commander Urban paced the small room, frown deeply entrenched. The Commander's office did not look too much different from Tanni's own quarters, except that this room had the space for a desk with two sides - though she had never seen Emily sit behind it, and the sleeping space was obscured by an accordion divider. Otherwise, it was the same beige-painted steel walls of the rest of Venusberg. It was rectangular and cramped and made Tanni long to be back with her drones, back in the wide open spaces of the planet's surface.

"Well, no," she started, attempting to explain for what felt like the hundredth time, though only because she'd gone over the conversation in her head so many times before reporting. "It was faster than the specs I had been given. The documentation showed the same top speed for the new drone model as for the model I was already using, so I didn't anticipate the speed."

"So, on day one, the newest drone on our roster overshoots the work area by a few hundred feet, runs into an exposed electrical feed, and was stranded down there on the surface?"

"Yes."

"And then it just disappeared?"

"I scanned for it this morning and even sent another drone out to the area to look for it, but it's not there anymore."

"It just vanished? Was it buried? Was it dragged away? Did it walk away on its own? Drones don't just *disappear.*"

"I couldn't get close enough to investigate further. I didn't want..." she paused there, *didn't want it to be seen*, was the answer. "I didn't want to risk another drone in the same area," she said instead.

Emily continued to pace, her tan suit and pale skin and hair blending in well with the beige environment of the citystation, like she was part of Venusberg itself, a sharp contrast with Tanni, whose coppery skin and chalk-blue jumpsuit stood out from everything around her.

"Why didn't you report the malfunction right away last night?"

"I thought I could handle it myself in the morning."

"And that's the whole story?" The question wasn't accusing, or at least didn't seem so to Tanni. For a moment, she was tempted to tell the rest of what happened. Emily was a friend, she would understand. Considering, Tanni looked her manager directly in the eyes, and saw Emily Urban as she *really* was: part of the machine. The station itself was like a drone, working at the behest of The Triad Corporation. She and Emily were just parts of that machine, components to be manipulated from afar by a controller they never saw or really knew.

Tanni looked away from her superior's angry frown, looking first at the floor, then at the controller's desk. She could see the corner of the recessed monitor in the surface of the workstation. The readout at the bottom of the screen indicated that it was following EnMa-1, but she couldn't see where it was or what it was doing from this angle. Emily was not her friend or even her boss. Emily was the antennae, and Tanni was a clawed appendage, a broken, clawed appendage. If the controller discovered her malfunction, she'd have to be repaired. "Yes," she lied, "that's everything."

"Well, with the scope on your feed still down, we have no record to look over, so I guess I have no choice but to accept that explanation."

Tanni didn't look away from the desk. "It's what happened."

"Tanni," Tanni felt a slim hand grip her shoulder and then Emily's body was blocking the view of the screen. She had moved around in front of the desk and was before her now, one foot on the floor and the other dangling, as she half sat on the front of her desk. Her frown had flattened and widened, a sympathetic and understanding line, which was somehow worse than the angry frown. "Victoria," Tanni was startled at the sound of her own first name. She didn't think that Emily had called her that since her first day on the job. Was it meant to be comforting or ominous? "You're our best controller," she continued. "I can't afford to lose you, quite literally. The expense to train and emigrate a replacement for you is prohibitive at this point, so you shouldn't fear for your job yet, but you need to be more careful."

Yet. Tanni looked back down at the tiled floor. She was an *expensive,* broken, clawed appendage then. Emily pulled her hand away, shifting her weight fully up onto the front of the desk. "Yes," Tanni said. "I'm sorry, Emily."

"I don't know what happened to you yesterday, if it was lack of sleep or hunger or... whatever, but this wouldn't have happened if you weren't distracted." Emily said. "I'm going to have to explain this to the board. You don't have to worry about them, that's my concern, but I'll have to put you on personal rest for a few days and on probation for the next year, and there is no way I'll be able to get you another replacement."

"I understand."

Emily's face was suddenly stern again. "If something like this happens again, budget concerns won't help you, the board will want you off the project and out of Venusberg."

Tanni didn't say anything to this. She got up and moved toward the door.

"Tanni..." Emily called after her, voice softening, "take the next couple days to get your head together, okay?"

"Yeah." Tanni closed the door behind her and turned toward her own cabin.

Tanni was working on affixing the seal to the outer door of an airlock on Beta Column. It was a job that EnTa-3 could easily have done on its own, but she liked getting into the work. It was good to work with her hands, even if they weren't really her hands doing the work, and none of the other drones needed her attention right now. She paused to roll through the inputs of the other four drones, a habit she'd gotten into over the last few weeks since returning to work. She'd been more efficient in that time and had received praise from the commander for how well she'd recovered. Even some of the other controllers noticed her uptick. They still occasionally made fun for her having lost a second drone in as many months, though none of them blamed her for the accident that took out EnTa-2 and damaged the command center's scope, and none of them knew the circumstances of the loss of EnTa-7.

Perhaps Emily was right: she had just needed a break from everything.

When she had gotten back to her cabin that day, she had collapsed and slept straight through for two Earth days, then spent a shift eating ravenously and writing letters to people back on Earth, people she'd regretted having lost contact with over the years, before sleeping another 10 hours. She returned revitalized and recuperated, and, she dared say, she returned happy. Occasionally, her mind forced her to replay the events of that night, but mostly she was able to convince herself that she must have been imagining everything.

She didn't have to roll to EnTa-1. She could see it down the interior hallway, still painting. Enta-4 was repairing a fan unit which had arrived damaged in the *RapUnsEl* this morning. EnTa-5 was climbing Delta Column where EnTa6 was waiting for help lifting a panel into place.

Tanni rolled back to EnTa-3 and continued installing the massive pressure seal. She had placed only two more rivets when she saw a green light flash at the upper limit of her vision, the sign that a drone was activating. Had one of the units needed to restart? She selected the feed with a flick and rolled to the unit.

EnTa-7.

Her lost drone was coming online!

The view was just as black as the last moments of her previous session with the drone, but slowly, the camera was coming online and adjusting to the environment. Fuzzy at first, she saw only what looked like a steel grating over a dirt surface. The camera was pointed down at a floor somewhere. Had it been stolen? It had to still be within the range of the control tower, so it couldn't have gone far.

Tanni switched into direct control mode and shrugged into the drone. She felt the awkwardness of her control of it once again, and vertigo, or the memory of vertigo, threatened to overwhelm her. Slowly, she looked up, focusing the camera on the area in front of her. Someone was standing there, facing away from her at a workbench.

Dark, wavy hair tied back into a pony-tail above a slim, lab coated form. The dancer!

He turned slightly, looking over his shoulder, one piercing amber eye looking directly at her, eyebrow raised. "Ah!" he exclaimed and then turned back to his workbench for a moment before turning around to face her. "You're okay!" His face held a child-like excitement, which sat strangely on his narrow features. He was definitely the same man that Tanni had seen through the domed glass that night, but here, in this setting, he was not as beautiful, not as mesmerizing. In his hands, he held an MPU board and one of the forward access panels for the drone. The panel was scorched and bent, the MPU had dots of fresh solder. "I didn't expect you to activate on your own… or, I mean… I didn't expect *your drone* to reactivate on *its* own…" his brow furrowed. "This is a drone, right?"

A bit stunned, Tanni nodded her head slightly, the motion transferring to the camera of the drone. The man looked relieved then, again a very child-like expression. "I thought so!" he said. "The way your antennae - I mean, your drone's antennae - and processors are configured, I could only imagine that it was being controlled from a distant place, probably the citystation via the main data tower, right? Or do you use the skyhook itself to transmit?" he looked at her a moment considering, then answered himself. "No, that would be too slow, of course. It must be the data tower." Tanni nodded again.

He took a step toward her with the parts still in hand and bent down in front of her, his face coming very close to the camera. She saw slight freckles, light against the darkness of his sharp cheekbones. "Do you mind if I slip in this last board?" he asked but did not wait for an answer. She watched his eyes as he reached down, and she felt very exposed just then, as the man clicked the MPU board into place and then screwed the panel closed — from her perspective, about where her belly button would be. His eyes narrowed while he concentrated, and for a moment, she saw the intensity that had drawn her to him two weeks ago. It passed as quickly as it had come, and his boyishness shone through again.

"There," he said, standing up after the panel snapped into place, "you should be able to move around again now." He smiled, broadly and toothily down at her. "Go ahead. Put it through its paces."

Tanni's shock was wearing off and she found herself indignant instead. She felt condescended to, embarrassed, *violated*. "How dare you!?" she nearly screamed at him. He didn't react. He simply continued to smile at her, eagerly. She realized that the drone's speaker was still off. She switched it on. "What were you thinking?" she heard the sound of her own anger bounce off the walls of the small workshop. She didn't realize she'd been so angry, but it had been building up since her meeting with Emily two weeks ago. Anger with herself, anger at the situation, anger at Venus. Now it had a real target. Now she had someone to really blame. He looked confused and a bit crestfallen. He looked around nervously. *Did he really not understand what he had done?*

"You stole a drone from The Triad Corporation! You almost got me fired! The entire organization thinks I'm some kind of half-wit! And you stand there smug and patronizing, pleased with yourself as if you've done me a favor?!" His mood changed quickly, and he slumped to the floor in front of her. He looked down and away, his hands and face trembling.

"I'm sorry," he said. She thought he might cry at any moment. "I just thought…" he stammered. "I was trying to help. When I saw what happened, I knew I could fix it. I had to fix it. I didn't… I didn't think…"

As she watched the handsome man sputter his apology, she began to feel terrible. "Look," she said finally, trying to make her voice soft, "It's… all right."

He looked up. There were tears in his eyes. *Dammit.* "What are you going to do?"

She wasn't sure how to answer that question. What *should* she do? Take this drone back outside and start working again, like nothing had happened? How would she explain that? What story would she tell?

Instead of answering, she asked, "Who are you?"

The man's face brightened as fast as it had dimmed. He stood quickly and gracefully. The remaining hints of tears made his eyes shine in the bright workshop lights. "Sam Rampion," he said. "Director of Venusian Botanical Research for Türme Industries." He held out a hand to her as if to shake, then looked down at it sheepishly, and used it instead to gesture out at the dome beyond the open door of the workshop. "Out there is my garden."

Tanni moved one of the drone's appendages out toward Sam and opened the small, padded claw on the end. He looked at it for a moment with a furrowed brow, then smiled broadly, taking the claw in his hand and shaking it. "Victoria Tannhauser," she said.

"Victoria," he said, repeating her name as if to commit it to memory. "Do people call you 'Vicky?'"

"No," she said, cringing, "people actually just call me 'Tanni.'"

"Very well, Tanni." He gestured toward the door of the workshop again. "May I give you the tour?"

Tanni glanced in the direction of the door. What would it hurt? At the least it would give her something to do while she figured out how she was going to handle this. She quickly scanned the feeds for her other drones. EnTa-3 was still just staring at the airlock seal, riveter mid-way to the next contact point. "Hang on just a second," she said. Sam pulled his feet together, gripped his hands behind his back, and nodded, looking serious, like she was a visiting dignitary, and he a lowly tour guide.

She cut off direct control of EnTa-7 and rolled over to EnTa-3. The difference in perspective jarring her slightly. *What am I going to do?* she asked herself as she started on a set of commands that would allow EnTa-3 to work without her input for a while. *I can't just tell Emily "Oh, sorry, I forgot to mention there was also this hot, botanist dancer in a dome, and it turns out he kidnapped my drone so he could repair it after he caught me spying on him."* She laughed at the situation finally, feeling a bit of tension slip away as she coded the final commands and then watched for a moment longer to ensure the drone was following her orders before rolling back to EnTa-7 and reestablishing direct control.

Sam was still in the position she had left him, but when he saw the drone begin to move again, he smiled and dropped his hands to his sides. "Okay," she said, "I'm ready to see your garden."

Tanni was laying out orders for EnTa-1 to ascend to the top of Beta Column from the inside to get at a support beam that EnTa-4 was having trouble installing on its own when she heard Sam's voice.

"Hey, Tanni?" Over the last few months, she'd taken to leaving the audio channel open on EnTa-7 so that Sam could talk to her whenever he wanted. It meant that she also often overheard him talking to colleagues over the net about a current project (he only rarely got actual visitors) or sometimes singing to himself in the workshop. When she heard him start up the music for one of his ballet routines, she would always find a way to watch. He claimed to be shy about having an audience, but since she wasn't *really* there, it didn't bother him as much. In fact, he seemed to revel in the attention. Last time the *RapUnsEl* had come down to the surface, there had been a package on it for him, which he had been eager to show her: a real leotard, like professional dancers wore. She felt bad that it had probably cost him quite a bit to get it sent all the way out here - space on the bimonthly cargo ship to Venus was at a premium - but she had to admit that it made his performances all the more impressive.

"Tanni?" she glanced at the feed from EnTa-7 and saw Sam's face, far too close to the camera. She could see only one eye and some freckles.

She chuckled and switched on her mic. "Yes, Sam?"

"I hate to ask, but would you be free to assist me in the garden?"

"I'll be there in just a minute," she said and switched the mic back off. Sam's face disappeared. And was replaced by the view of his garden, which she typically left EnTa-7 pointed at while using a nearby power node to keep its batteries charged. Currently the plants were all bathed in the glow of the dome's artificial sunlight, much brighter than the view she was getting from her other drones, mostly out in the darkness of the moonless Venusian night, which would last another few weeks, Earth time.

She knew that Sam had machines to help him with his work in the garden: diggers and lifters and so forth; she'd seen him use them before. But she didn't mind helping out – it wasn't like it cost her anything - and she enjoyed chatting with him. Typically, he would chatter on about botany, which didn't particularly interest her, but other times he would talk about his love of the arts, or he would ask her questions about herself. She often got so absorbed with pleasant conversation that she would completely forget that she was not actually there in the garden with him. She had become more acclimated to EnTa-7's systems, and her clumsiness with the unit was gone. Of all her drones, it was the one that felt the most like an extension of her own person. Of course, that was by design.

She finished with EnTa-1 and rolled right into direct control mode for EnTa-7.

Looking around, she didn't see Sam immediately, but she heard his voice faintly from the far side of the dome by the airlocks. "Yes sir," he was saying, "but I have to work with the soil and sunlight I have, there is only so much I can-"

"Rampion," another voice began, sharply, "I brought you here because I thought you could deliver for this project on our timeline." She recognized the voice but wasn't sure from where. The person was in the dome though, not on a net connection.

"It should be working," Sam said. "If we were on Earth, I could fill the quota twice over."

"Well, we're not on Earth," the voice shot back at Sam, and she sympathized with him. She recognized an upbraiding from a boss when she heard one. "That's the whole point! Anyone could grow this stuff on Earth. We need it grown here!"

"Yes, Sir, Mr. Türme. *Mr. Türme!* Tomas Türme? No wonder she recognized the voice! She'd heard it hundreds of times in news vids, though she'd never heard him angry. While they spoke, she sneaked past a small bush, to the edge of the workshop enclosure, and peeked a camera around the corner toward the airlock.

"The timeline of the entire project has to be pushed back because of your delays," Türme's voice grew a bit softer. "You understand the importance of the project, don't you, son?"

"Yes, Sir."

"Good man. I know you're doing your best here, and I must say that your garden is quite beautiful."

"Thank you, sir," Sam said. She could hear the smile in his voice, but she couldn't actually see either of the figures through the trees; just their shoes were visible. "Can I show you around?"

A pause then. "No, I've got other appointments to keep." The nicer shoes moved toward the open airlock. "A revised schedule will be sent to you. Do try to stick to it, will you?"

"Yes, sir."

"Good man, Rampion." And then the airlock closed, and Sam turned away from it, walking back toward her. She pulled back to her usual resting place.

"Sorry about that," Sam said when he came down the path and saw that she was in control of EnTa-7 - he always seemed to be able to tell right away.

"It's okay," Tanni said. "Was that Tomas Türme, I heard?" "Yeah." Sam looked sheepish.

"You work directly for Tomas Türme? One of the most powerful men in the Solar System?" Tanni nearly screeched. Türme was the CEO and sole owner of the largest private company in human history. Türme Corp had its hands in nearly every business one could think of, except building and managing extra-terran surface stations. One of the reasons The Triad Corporation was still able to compete so well in extra-terran construction was because Türme was unwilling to pursue it. "Why didn't you ever tell me?"

Sam shrugged. "It never came up."

Tanni gave Sam a squinting look before remembering that he couldn't see her face. "What is he even doing on Venus?" she asked. "Isn't he a staunch anti-terraformer?"

Sam nodded. "I guess he sees the advantage in having a few domes here."

"What project was he talking about?"

"I…" he stumbled over his words, "I'm basically the entire Venusian Botanical Research Department." He was looking toward the airlock with apprehension. Or was it fear? Tanni wanted to know more but decided it best to ask about it later.

"Sorry," she said, "I'm being nosey. What did you call me over for?"

"Oh, yes!" Sam exclaimed, forgetting the tension of a moment ago. I need to move this tree over to here," he said, pointing first at a small pine, then at a hole big enough for its root ball. "I did all the digging and cutting already, I just still need to move it, and I thought you might help with that." "Is that all I am to you?" Tanni said playfully. "A forklift?"

"Of course not!" Sam smiled. "You're also my pretty robot friend and the president of my very small fan club."

Tanni felt herself blush and was grateful that he couldn't see her. "How would you know if I'm pretty? You've never even seen me."

"I have that one photograph you sent me," he said with a smirk as she carried the tree past him, "the one with the giant hair."

Ugh. She should never have sent him that photo, but it was the only one she'd had handy, and she'd wanted him to have a face to go with her voice, so he'd stop thinking of her as EnTa-7 - or "Entat," as he had taken to calling the drone. The photo had been taken in college, when she'd been younger and fitter, but she'd also had a giant, double-puffball hair-do. They were in fashion at the time, but now it looked a bit dated.

She dropped the tree, a bit too roughly, into the designated hole, and Sam squeezed past her to steady it with one hand and keep it from toppling. "Sorry!" she said.

He smiled down into her camera, face very close to the lens once again. "Too bad you're not my *graceful* robot friend," he said with a smirk, then took a step back to look at where the tree was. "I hate to have to move a tree like that," he said, picking up a small needley twig that had fallen to the steel decking around the tree's new place, "but this one was never really supposed to be over there anyhow, and it was too close to the irrigation pipes."

"Uh huh," Tanni said absently. EnTa-1 was notifying her that it had completed her task and was waiting for new orders. Tanni turned and started back toward the corner where EnTa-7 usually sat. "Is that all you needed help with?" she asked as she moved away.

"Yes, thank you," he said.

"No problem."

"Tanni?"

She stopped and turned the camera around. "Yeah?"

"Have you told your boss yet?"

This again… "No," she said and sighed heavily.

"You really should." He looked concerned.

"I know," she said, almost whining, "I just haven't figured out how yet."

Sam shrugged. "You know it's just going to be worse the longer-"

"I know, Sam," she cut him off. It wasn't the first time they'd had this very exchange. "Just please, let me figure this out, okay?"

Sam raised his hands before him in surrender, but she could see his frown.

She sighed again and shook her head. She had work to do. Sam was still looking at her when she turned away, and in moments, she was at the top of Beta Column, lifting an awkward steel beam into place.

Tanni watched casually as Sam leaped and spun and landed gracefully next to a small berry bush. It always seemed like his momentum would take him clear off of the platform, but in the year she'd been watching him, he'd never stepped one toe off of the steel grating. For the last month, he'd been practicing *The Nutcracker*, and the music flowed through the greenhouse dome tinily. She had offered once to help him improve the acoustics in the structure, but there had been no good way to do it without blocking some of the valuable sunlight, made more valuable recently by the completion of a nearby arcology that put Sam's garden in the shade for a tenth of each Venusian day. He was able to make up the difference with artificial sunlight, but it was still less than ideal, and the plants already struggled enough having to grow under artificial lights for two months at a time during the night.

Tanni's own construction project was nearing completion as well. She was the only controller who hadn't been moved yet onto a new project from the envi plant as it neared completion, and it had taken some convincing. Emily had been shocked that Tanni wanted to remain on the project when the only tasks left were mostly automated operations setting up living quarters and kitchens and such for the people who would live in and operate the tower - the sorts of tasks that Tanni typically tried to avoid. Other controllers were happy to move on, however, so Tanni was left to finish up the project. Another few days, and she'd need to move on as well, and she might lose access to the local control tower when that happened.

EnTa-6 blinked at her. It was finished putting doors onto a row of habitation modules. She rolled away from EnTa-7 to give the drone new orders while still glancing at the feed occasionally to catch glimpses of Sam. Carefully, she lined up the simple orders required to get the desks attached to the walls in each of these rooms. She couldn't help but imagine the men and women who would soon live here, currently on their way from Earth. They'd arrive at Venusberg in only a couple months, and afterward, they would live here in these very rooms for perhaps years, looking at these doors, these desks, these beds, these rivets every day, never knowing her, who had put it all together for them. A wobbly desk now could mean years of annoyance for the resident, much more important to their day-to-day lives than any given exterior panel or support cable. These anonymous things would soon be very personal to someone. She double checked her list of orders when she was finished, trying to think of a way to do something more expressive, something that would have an impact on the people who lived there, but she couldn't think of anything, so she started EnTa-6 on its way and rolled back over to EnTa-7 and shrugged in to catch the end of Sam's dance.

Sam went from a short sauté into a fluttering about en pointe before coming to a stop with a flourishing plié. He'd been explaining some of the basics of ballet to her over the months, but she still didn't really get what it all meant, she just enjoyed watching him do it.

"Hey!" Tanni called out when he didn't move again, "wasn't that Marie's part?"

He lifted his head and laughed his easy, melodic laugh. "Just seeing if you were paying attention," he quipped. "Besides, how am I supposed to keep from mixing the parts up if I don't have anyone to dance with? While you were fiddling with your drones a minute ago, I almost picked myself up and tossed myself into a cactus."

"You don't even have any cactus," she said, playing along.

"I do have someone here who could be my dance partner, though." He straightened back up and stretched a hand out to her, beckoning.

"I don't think you can lift Entat," she said and laughed at the image in her head while moving toward the platform.

"That's okay, you can be the prince, and I'll be Marie."

"I don't know if I believe you as the maiden in distress," she said. "Besides, we'd have to put some thicker pads on my claws."

"I trust you not to snip me in half."

Tanni stopped the drone before Sam and held out one appendage. Sam took the claw in his hand and bowed with a deep flourish, his face coming close to the camera. Tanni tried to bow also, but nearly lost control, and felt her gyros kick in to pull her back up as a brief moment of vertigo overtook her.

Laughing, he knelt down in front of her, so his face was level with her cameras. "Let's start with an easier sort of dance, then." He took one of her claws and placed it on his shoulder, moving that hand to the side of EnTa-7, about where her waist would be. Then, he held her other appendage out to the side, and drew close. Stunned, she stared directly into his bright eyes and watched the sunlight dance there and glisten off of the sweat that trickled down across his dark cheeks. She swallowed hard and blinked away her own sweat. She had mostly gotten over the way he made her feel, settling into a warm friendship with this beautiful dancer over their months together, but there were some moments...

"Perhaps you should lead?" he said suddenly, his smile curving into the familiar smirk, and she realized that she'd been just staring, while he had been trying to take small shuffling movements with his kneepads against the platform

"Oh no!" she said. "It's like my junior prom all over again!"

"Ha!" he barked a sharp laugh.

"You think I'm joking."

"I know you're not," he said, not unkindly. "Now lead."

Sighing, she made a small, unconfident step to one side, and then shuffled the other leg beside it. Sam followed smoothly, despite his awkward position. She took another small step, then another, and soon they were turning small, slow circles there on the steel platform, the *Nutcracker Suite* still playing throughout the glowing dome above them, Sol shining down upon the two of them through the twisting atmosphere of an alien world. In this moment, she felt closer to him than she had anyone in many long years, but as she sat fifty thousand kilometers above the surface in her beige box in Venusberg, she also felt so very far away from everyone. She longed only to lay her head against Sam's shoulder and to draw him close to her body. She wanted to feel his muscled form under her hands and for him to feel her narrow waist under his.

"It's too bad," he said, once they had found a rhythm,

"that I can't visit you in Venusberg to dance with you there."

"I was just thinking the same thing," she said. "Can't you come up for a visit?"

"How would you explain to your co-workers how we even know each other?" he asked, smirking again. "Besides, my

contract keeps me pretty well stuck in this lab."

20

"You don't get any vacation?"

He looked away from her. "The contract I signed with Türme didn't include many provisions or benefits."

"Is that legal?" she asked as she turned his face into the sunlight again.

He shrugged. "I guess I didn't really think it was all that important at the time, but now…"

"You're trapped here?"

He nodded. "I can't leave this dome, much less the surface, without Türme's permission, and I don't have the resources to do anything. My payments are going to an account on Earth that I can't do anything with from here."

"There must be something that can be done. If I can help at all from Venusberg…"

"No!" he said sharply, almost stumbling. "You can't do anything. You can't tell anyone."

"What? Sam, I don't understand-" they had stopped dancing.

"You have to promise, Tanni."

"But I don't…"

"It could be very dangerous." He stood up then and turned away from her. "Mr. Türme is a powerful man and… Look, you need to promise!"

Tanni was stunned at his sudden turn. He was typically mercurial, but this was more dramatic than usual. "Okay, I promise, I- I'm sorry, I didn't mean..."

"Controller Tannhauser" It was Commander Urban. *Not now!*

"Sam, hang on a sec, okay," she said. Sam didn't turn around. Tanni switched voice channels, turning off EnTa7's speaker, and tuning to the command channel. "Emily, is this urgent?"

"Sorry to interrupt, Tanni," she said, "I just wanted to give you the good news that your command scope has been repaired."

"Oh…"

"Yeah, I get the feeling that this isn't good news for either of us."

"Sam…"

"I think you should worry about yourself here. Report to my office, please."

And with that, Tanni's connection to all of her drones was severed, and she was left in the dark with that ominous "Connection Lost" message floating in red before her.

"Oh no…"

INTERIM - WITCH AND POPE

The call was taking longer than expected to connect. "Waiting for remote party," was all the screen said.

Tanni didn't remember a lot of the meeting that had immediately followed the discovery of her… *indiscretions*. That was Emily's word for what had been going on. There had been a lot about the "monumental waste of resources" and the "unprecedented breach of trust," but the Commander's anger and her lack of forgiveness or understanding now just blended into an uncomfortable memory. Most of the words, especially Tanni's own, were lost.

Afterward, Tanni had been booked on the next ship off Venus aboard the S.S. *Einstein*. How she was going to pay for the trip, she had no idea. The Triad Corporation had paid for her trip from Earth to Venus five years ago, but they weren't paying for her to be shipped home, nor would they allow her to stay in Venusberg. She was gone from that place forever. She would never even work in the industry again, much less ever connect with her drones again, or see Sam.

Oh, Sam…

She hadn't even said goodbye to him. He wouldn't even know what had happened to her. She had tried to find a way to send him a message, but she could find no way to get in touch with him away from the Venusian data tower. He wasn't even in the Türme Industries employee directory.

Tanni bit her lip nervously and looked over to the well-dressed man at her left elbow. His dark hair slicked back, his dark suit crisp at the edges. He had a strong bearing of authority, but when he saw her looking over at him, he smiled disarmingly. She tried to smile back but wasn't sure it came through.

A day ago, this man had pulled her from her cabin on the *Einstein*. "A matter of security," was all he would explain as he took her to the airlock, where another ship was waiting. At first, she thought the ship was being evacuated due to some emergency, but then she realized that she was the only one who had been moved. She still didn't know the name of the man nor the ship. He had since only said that she was to take a call from the chairman. Did the chairman of The Triad Corporation really need to reprimand her personally? Did she need to be on a different ship to take the call? She could have talked to her from her tiny cabin on the *Einstein*. Did Triad even have the authority to tell her where to go, and who to take calls from anymore? Didn't they just fire her?

She had to admit that despite all the questions, she was glad to be out of that cabin after nearly a week of boredom and solitude. She had completely run out of movies to watch and news to read, and the journey wasn't half over. Constant thought of Sam and her drones didn't help the time pass either. She didn't relish the thought of going back to the cabin after this call, so perhaps it was okay that it was taking so long.

As if to betray her, the message finally changed to "Connecting." She straightened up before the screen as a man came into focus on the other side of a small desk. Wait...wasn't the Chairman of Triad a woman? She recognized this man though...

"Oh..." she said when she recognized him, *that Chairman.*

"Victoria Tannhauser?" the man asked.

"Yes, sir," Tanni said.

"This is Chairman Frederick Holland of the Sol Council," he said unnecessarily. "I apologize for the abrupt and unexplained nature of this call."

"That's okay, sir. Um..." What do you say to The Chairman? The most powerful man in the system? "It's good to meet you?" is what came out.

"I'm glad to meet you, Ms. Tannhauser," he replied. He seemed warmer, more congenial than in the news vids.

She glanced to her left. Was this really happening?

"I'll get right to the point," he said, smiling a bit sadly. "You seem to have stumbled upon something of great importance while you were working on Venus, and the Sol Council would like more information and possibly your assistance, if you're willing."

"Of course."

"Great," he said, a bit too exuberantly. "The gentleman there with you is Agent Weaver. You'll be working with him going forward."

She looked over at Weaver, who smiled again. "Working on what?" she said to both of them.

"I'll leave that for Agent Weaver to explain," The Chairman said. "Thank you for your assistance, Ms.

Tannhauser."

"Umm… Bye," she said, feeling confused and a bit lame.

The feed cut off.

Tanni turned to Agent Weaver. She felt like she should have been angry, but she was just so glad that she hadn't been yelled at again that she didn't feel up to being indignant. "So," she started, "where am I?"

"We're on the *Tesla*," Weaver said.

The *Tesla?* But it wasn't one of the other ships leaving Venus recently. That means… "We're not on our way to Earth, are we?"

"No, Tanni," he said, still smiling. "We're turning you around." He stood then and gestured for her to follow.

"Why?" she asked. "Does this have something to do with Sam?"

"It has everything to do with Mr. Rampion," he said as he turned and left the room.

Tanni had no choice but to follow if she wanted more answers. In the tiny passageway outside, he led her to another part of the ship's gravity ring, through two bulkheads, and into a meeting room of sorts before he spoke again.

"How well do you know Samuel Rampion?"

"Is he in trouble?" she asked in response. "Is he some kind of criminal?"

Weaver sighed, as if in resignation. Though his smile didn't falter, it developed a bit of a crook. "We don't quite know what to think yet, but it's possibly very significant that Rampion is on Venus." He paused here, seeming to consider. "I suppose you won't be much help until you know what's going on?" he said it like a question, but didn't wait for her to answer. "Rampion is suspected to be a member of the ATaPH League. You know what that is?"

Tanni nodded, slowly, wide eyed. The Anti Terraforming and Planetary Habitation movement was small but politically loud. She'd heard some news reports that a radical faction had been responsible for some attacks on the Martian colony a few years back. "Why would an ATaPH supporter be living and working on the surface?" she asked, confused.

"That's exactly what we're worried about. It's especially concerning that he's working in a facility that seems to be personally owned by Tom Türme, a major backer of the ATaPH, and possibly the leader of the radical ATaPH league."

"Oh, no…"

"Our records show that Samuel Rampion was killed during a demonstration on Earth five years ago," he continued, ignoring her exclamation and worried look, "and we don't know how he would have gotten to Venus undetected, but you seem to have found him there."

How could this be true? Samuel was so kind, so innocent, and she's supposed to believe he's what… *a terrorist*? "There must be another explanation," she said.

"We need to know what he's planning," Weaver continued, patiently, "and how he's getting his orders from Türme."

She was about to tell him about having seem Türme on the surface eight months ago when the implications of what he was saying hit her first. "You want me to spy on him for you," she said, surprised at her matter-of-factness.

"In a manner of speaking, yes," Weaver said, smiling at her understanding, "but we have a week before we get back to Venus, and there is more I would like to know."

Tanni slumped in the chair, defeated by the shock of all of this. Later, she knew, she would be angry, she would be indignant, she would be terrified, but now she was only numb.

PART TWO - SILK AND WORSHIP

Darkness.

Tanni was back with her drones on the warped surface of Venus, but it was not the comfort she thought it would be. The work she was having them do was meaningless. The envi plant had been completed by another operator while she was gone for two weeks, but she needed a cover, a reason to keep her work in the area, so her drones were being made busy. EnTa-1 and 3 were both just climbing to the tops of columns, waiting a short interval, and then descending and moving to another tower to repeat the performance. EnTa4 and 6 were stripping and repainting external components. She was building a program for EnTa-5 to loosen and retighten every bolt on the outside of Beta Column. EnTa-7 was still dark. She'd been glancing over to EnTa-7's feed every few minutes since she had put the control helmet back on that morning. The drone was active, but the view was black.

Any joy at reuniting with her drones was dampened by their useless activity and her new oversight. The repaired scope was not under surveillance from Emily, though that would have also been difficult. It was Agent Weaver who watched her every move and spoke quietly in her ear. She'd spent a lot of time with the quiet man over the last week, going over every detail she could remember about her time with Sam and especially the visit Türme had made to the garden. Weaver had spent an entire day trying to tease more out of her regarding that five-minute conversation.

Tanni glanced toward the western horizon, where the sun was near setting, a process that took more than a week and caused the sky to glow a brilliant grapefruit red with just traces of bright blues and greens swirled throughout. In another few earth days, the bottom of the bright disc of Sol would kiss the distant ridges, and in a mere 13 hours, would sliver and disappear, though the bright glow in the western sky would take days to fade.

"Tanni," Weaver's voice popped into her head. He didn't bother providing a visual to her, the way Emily always had. "I need you to switch to Entat now." He had started calling EnTa-7 by the name Sam used, after he'd heard about it. It made Tanni uncomfortable.

"I'm not finished yet with this program. You-"

"Now, Tanni." His voice was soft as usual; urgent, but not commanding.

She pulled out of command mode for EnTa-5 and rolled over to EnTa-7.

Darkness.

"There is something going on there," Weaver said.

Then Tanni heard it too: muffled voices. "Someone is talking nearby."

"Yes. I want you to get into a better position to listen."

Tanni shrugged into the drone and tried to look around for any light, the texture of the darkness slid past her view.

She reached up one appendage and could see it faintly before her. "I've been covered with a tarp or something," she said.

"Can you remove it?"

"I'm working on it." She closed the claw, gripping the covering, and pulled it down. It slid easily over her and crinkled as it fell to the ground in front of her. She cringed at the noise, but the conversation going on nearby did not change in tone. Looking around, she saw close walls and a number of tools on pegs. "I'm in one of the tool sheds." She couldn't help but giggle a bit at an image of Sam struggling to lift EnTa-7 off the central platform and into a shed.

"Concentrate, Tanni," Weaver gently admonished.

"Sorry."

"I still can't hear the conversation well, can you get closer without being seen?"

"I'm not sure," she admitted. "I don't know which shed this is, or which way it faces."

"Well, try to get out there, but be careful."

"Sure thing, boss," she said, going for sardonic but ending up at nervous instead.

Tanni slowly, carefully lifted the latch bar on the door with one claw while moving her camera toward the seal. The door cracked slightly open, and Tanni could see out. The voices were suddenly much clearer, and she could see two forms at the distant airlock, where she had seen Sam talking to Türme once before. She could see Türme clearly this time, his narrow face animated, his gesturing hands angry. "I don't know how, dammit," he was saying, "but my source tells me that they're close, so we have to speed things up."

"Will we still have time to get off-world?" Sam sounded flat, perhaps a bit sad.

Tanni turned so that her microphone was pointed at the opening, then shut off DC mode so that EnTa-7 would remain perfectly still.

"Of course," Türme said. "The next elevator departure is in one week, and we will be on it, just in time to get away from this wretched place before it all goes to hell, but not if you back out on me. This last batch of Supernitrates will ensure we make a lasting impression on the Sol

Government, even if it won't be as... *dramatic* as our original plan."

"Yeah."

Türme reached out a hand and placed it on Sam's shoulder. Tanni still could not see Sam's face, but she saw him tense up at the touch. "Look, Rampion, I know you never really agreed with this plan, but you have seen the same big picture I have, and you must understand that this is the only way." Türme smiled toothily. "Future generations will remember us as heroes, will see this as a turning point in the fight to untether ourselves from planets and move out to the stars."

Almost imperceptibly, Sam nodded.

"All right, then. Get back to work," Türme said as he released Sam's shoulder and turned to leave. "The movement needs your magic compounds!" Then the slim man was out of the dome, the airlock hissing into a cycle.

As soon as Türme was out of sight, Tanni shrugged back into EnTa-7.

"What are you doing?" Weaver asked.

"I've got to go talk to him, he's obviously here under duress."

"Yes, but we need a plan first. Things like this can get very complicated."

Tanni sighed, and, reluctantly, closed the shed's door before rolling back to EnTa-5. "Doesn't seem very complicated," she said. "We've got to get Sam out of there."

"He may be a victim of ATaPH's plans, but he's not entirely innocent. He may be reluctant to cooperate with us.

We need to be careful how we approach this."

"Perhaps," she said, "but I think I know how we can get him away from Türme." She was looking through a window of Delta column, into the vacant living quarters.

When Tanni finally rolled back to EnTa-7, it was late evening, settlement time. The drone was still in the shed, and she listened for a moment before opening the door. When she swung it out, she found herself irrationally hoping to catch him in a dance, but there was no music, no flashing leotard, no Sam. She moved out of the shed and onto the main platform and looked around. The garden glowed with the ruby light of the setting sun, every facet of the dome above her a glittering gemstone.

Sam moved out of his workshop, face fallen, lab coat hanging on drooping shoulders. He turned and spotted Tanni, and his face brightened. "Oh, Tanni!" he called. "I thought you had left me forever."

"I couldn't do that," she said in mock effrontery.

"I figured you'd been caught here with me and been fired for it," he said. "I thought I'd never see you again!"

He had walked briskly over to where she had positioned herself on the platform and knelt before her.

She said, "Well, I *was* fired, but then I was brought back."

"I'm sorry I yelled at you that day," he said frowning. "I thought I'd never be able to apologize for how abrupt I was." "It's okay Sam, I understand now."

He smiled then, but it quickly turned to concern. "What do you mean? *What* do you know?"

"We know Türme has you trapped here," she said. "We know you're not part of his plan voluntarily."

"Who is *we*? Who sent you back here?" he looked on the verge of anger. *Oops!* This was not going as well as she'd hoped. Weaver had been right, this was more delicate than she had thought it would be.

"An agent of the Sol Government is here with me," she started, gently. "He wants to help you and so do I."

He stood and turned away from her, reminding her of how she'd left him two weeks ago. "You can't be here. You and this agent need to leave me to my work. If you know why I'm here, then you know I have no choice."

Tanni hesitated. "Look," she said, going off script, "you don't have to commit to coming with me right now. It'll take a little while to get you out of here anyway, but you need to stop working on the supernitrates."

He turned back to her, finally returning to his normal slightly bemused demeanor, and sat half-lotus on the platform. "I can't. If I don't deliver the supernitrates, I don't think I'll make it off of Venus alive."

How could he be so blasé about this? "And if Türme does get the supernitrates, do you know what he'll do with them?" Sam only nodded, so Tanni continued. "He's building a bomb, isn't he?" Another nod. "Do you know his target?"

Sam sighed, as if in resignation. "The original plan was to bring down the three central arcologies, now I'm not so sure. Creating enough of the explosive to take down a building like that would take three batches of the supernitrates. I was supposed to have five done by now and deliver another four over the next year before the attack was to take place, but I underestimated how the sterile artificial environment would slow the bio activation process, and I'm just now almost done with the third batch." He gestured vaguely to an edge of the dome where five innocuous metal tanks of various sizes sat. Tanni had always assumed those were composters or fertilizer storage or something. She had been partly correct.

"But now that he knows he has been discovered, he's made a different plan?" she asked.

"Yes, but…" he shrugged, as if to say that none of this mattered. "I don't know what it is. He might be planning to take down just one arcology, or maybe he's changed to a completely different plan. I know it's not the envi plant, though he wishes it could be. I heard him say once that it would be too difficult to get the explosives to those columns, since they're not connected to the rest of the complex."

Just one arcology? Tanni thought. *That's still hundreds of colonists.* "What's the point of all this?" she asked.

"Politics," Sam said flatly. "At least it was originally. The idea on Mars three years ago was simple: create a destructive environment and drive people away, but the colony there was too well established, too entrenched to give up, so we turned to Venus. If we could demonstrate the weakness of surface colonies strongly enough, we'd save potentially thousands of human generations from the folly of terraforming." His calm air was fading again, this time in favor of passion. His eyes gleamed with the importance of his cause. "Tanni, do you know how wasteful it is to try to turn a whole planet to our own desires? How much fuel it takes to keep Venusberg stationary above a planet with such slow rotation?"

"Well, I-" she began, but he cut her off.

"Do you know how insecure the future of humanity is when it wastes what precious little energy and time it has trying to remake entire worlds?" he was nearly fanatical now in his insistence, but they honestly didn't sound like his words. "We should be exploring, expanding, building our cities among the stars, and forsaking the dirt of our ancestry. To do otherwise is stealing the future from our children and grandchildren!"

"Do you really believe all that, Sam?"

As quickly as he'd puffed up, he deflated. "I do," he said almost meekly, looking at the floor, "but it's gone too far, Tanni, and I can't get out."

Tanni took a step closer. "I can get you out," she said.

He looked back up at her and sighed. "What's your plan?"

"I'm going to get you a new suit," she said, smiling, though she knew he couldn't see, "then you're going to come stay in my tower."

Under cover of the violet Venusian sky, EnTa-3 approached the colony complex. The sun would reach the horizon in about twenty hours, but for now it tossed shadows long across the rocky ground. Tanni looked up and saw the vast gardens and steel bones of a massive arcology looming above her, green light cascading down onto the shadows of other structures. She turned along the base of the building and began to follow the perimeter of the complex toward Sam's dome. It was a longer route than just heading directly toward him, the way EnTa-7 had done that first night, but it made her journeys to and from the garden less conspicuous. EnTa-3 was slowed by the rough terrain but still managed almost 10 kph, so the remaining distance would be covered in about 15 minutes.

She was getting used to the route now. Tanni had run it every shift this week, bringing Sam parts of his suit. She passed a long, dark laboratory, and for a moment saw the drone's dim reflection in the thick glass walls. Legs pulled back, wheels down, today EnTa-3 was carrying a large, round helmet gripped in its appendages.

As she sped along the edge of the complex, Tanni considered the danger of what they were doing. She had been so excited by the risk and the challenge a few days earlier. It had felt like the turning point of some grand spy thriller, but as the days passed, and the real danger began to sink in, she only worried for Sam's safety, and, to some extent, felt bad that she was not actually in any danger herself, or at least it didn't feel like she was, being so far from the action. Agent Weaver had explained that getting involved in an operation against a powerful organization like ATaPH was always dangerous, but that was future-danger. Sam was in now-danger.

As EnTa-3 approached the outskirted dome, where she knew Sam was waiting, she slowed the drone to a more conservative pace and directed it to move right up to a point just a few meters from the exposed electrical feed that ran past the dome, and then she rolled over to EnTa-7.

"Okay, Sam," she said, turning to look at where he stood by an access panel in one of the arches of the dome, "lower your power grid."

He smiled his crooked smile and pressed a few buttons. He turned back to her and gave a thumbs-up. Tanni rolled back to EnTa-3 and nudged her way forward through where the unshielded conduit ran underground. "I'm clear", she said through EnTa-7, without switching away from control of EnTa-3. She heard the faint whine, an indication that the power had been brought back up, a sound that usually didn't register, just becoming part of the background of the dome. The power had only been down for a couple of seconds. Hopefully not long enough to register as anything other than a normal fluctuation to anyone monitoring the power usage out here.

EnTa-3 moved toward the emergency airlock in the dome, the same one Sam had dragged EnTa-7 in through over a year ago. The outer door opened, and Tanni brought EnTa-3 into it. She waited for the hiss of the airlock systems running through their cycles, then watched as the inside door opened, Sam standing behind it, lab coat swirling around him in the wind from the change in pressure. He must have run to get there in time, though, of course, he was not winded.

Tanni didn't think she had ever seen Sam out of breath. "This is the cutest one yet!" Sam called over his shoulder toward EnTa-7, though she heard him through EnTa-3's feed. "He's half the size of Entat."

He? She wondered how he chose the gender of the drone, all the others had been "she" so far. "You saying I'm fat?" she called out through EnTa-7.

"Yes," he called back playfully.

She heard Weaver groan then. She had forgotten that he was there.

Face growing hot, she stopped staring at Sam and moved EnTa-3 past him and into the dome, carrying the helmet toward the nearly complete suit she had been building for him. He followed behind and "hmmm"ed appreciatively as she set down the helmet next to the assembly. It wouldn't need to be attached until the rest of the suit was on Sam.

The suit itself resembled an old-timey submersible suit and with good reason. Out on the surface, getting oxygen was the easy part. The hard part was keeping from being crushed and burned. If it weren't for the atmospheric pressure and the heat, anyone could walk on the surface with just an oxygen tank on their hip. Someday, the terraforming would alleviate those issues, just as they had already removed the acids from the atmosphere.

"Almost finished," she told him, rolling EnTa-7 over to join them. She looked at EnTa-3 through EnTa-7's feed. She supposed that maybe he did look a bit small, though she still wouldn't say "cute." "All we need now is the recycler assembly." She pointed with one clawed appendage at a spot where a series of hoses and cables might attach.

"I'd feel a lot better if it was complete already," Sam said.

"Well, this is all that the engineers at the envi plant would ever need. The suit's own tank can hold enough air for about two hours, and if they had an issue that required more external time than that, they could send a drone." She turned to look up at Sam. "The recycler is on its way down on the *RapUnsEl* as we speak, accompanied by a small team of

Sol Government agents. When it arrives, I'll be there to meet it with EnTa-7."

He frowned then. "Can't one of the other drones go?" he asked. "It might be dangerous."

She sighed. "Entat is the fastest of the drones, and we... I would like to get the part from the elevator and back to you as fast as possible. Besides," she turned away, "it's no more dangerous for me to go with Entat than with any of the others."

"But Entat's the one I know," he said pitifully, "and she's the only one who can talk to me."

That was true, and she felt too, irrationally, that EnTa-7 was somehow more a part of her than the other drones, as though it carried a part of herself. She smiled; though she knew he could not see, it still gave a confident edge to her voice. "It'll be fine," she said, turning back to him again. "I'll only be out for a little while, and then you and Entat can run away together."

His smile returned then, reaching up to his eyes. She thrilled to look upon him when he was happy. His pleasure lit him up like no person she had ever seen. Though, as if in payment, his despair darkened the very air around him in his rare bad mood. In that moment, she wanted nothing more than to please him, to find a way to keep his smile on her forever.

"If you two are done goggling at each other..." Weaver prompted into her ear.

Tanni shook the reverie. "Right," she said, "Sam, let's go over the plan one more time. We only have another two days until the *RapUnsEl* touches down."

She moved EnTa-3 over into a corner and rolled directly into EnTa-7's DC mode as Sam turned and walked toward his lab, where he could sit while they talked. Tanni took one more glance at the suit, then moved after him.

"That's brilliant!" agent Weaver said in Tanni's ear. She looked down, confused, at the piece of sheet metal that EnTa-5 was bending back and forth needlessly.

"That's what sheet metal always does when you bend it too much." The busy work was mind-numbing, and it was getting difficult to think up new, useless assignments for the drones. At least it wouldn't be long, now.

"Not that," he said, "the *RapUnsEl.*"

"Oh," she said, then realized the implication. "OH!" The *RapUnsEl* was visible. It was almost time. She cancelled all the orders for her other drones and rolled over to EnTa-7. Its camera was pointed up at where the barely visible skyhook met the violet clouds, still illuminated by the sliver of the setting sun. She had ordered the drone to a spot near the base station a few hours ago, not knowing exactly when the *RapUnsEl* would arrive. Sometimes it was as much as a few hours early or late, and she wanted to be prepared. The elevator held the recycler which would complete Sam's suit and let him escape his garden prison.

The air warped. The ground shook.

Oh no... A fireball rose from the base station. The fire was strange and small compared to the effects of the explosion. Chunks of steel and plastic were tossed hundreds of yards in every direction. Smoke billowed out from the smoldering, shattered building, and the skyhook... flexed.

It was a slow movement at first, but it built into a whipping arc that tore the very air, screaming as it lashed out, as if grasping for another building to take it in. Tanni glanced up to the *RapUnsEl.* Smoke poured from the roof of the barge-like platform as the brakes engaged in an attempt to stop the freefall. The entire enclosure listed then, and the skyhook cable snapped above it with an immense crack that took several seconds to reach her on the ground. It was only then she realized that Weaver was trying to get her attention.

"-get the drone out of there, Tanni" she could hear him pleading after the terrible sound stopped bouncing through her head. "Move back!"

She listened. She turned around, and without looking back again toward the Skyhook and the falling *RapUnsEl,* Tanni and EnTa-7 ran.

The crash, when it came, was terrible. It wasn't loud. Tanni had expected it to be loud, but, of course, the speakers in her helmet limited the volume of the sound, but this, in a way, made it worse. She could hear the *RapUnsEl* crush against the surface in clear detail. She could pick out the sounds of crumpling metal and snapping cables distinctly.

There was the crash of breaking glass, the splintering of plastic cargo containers. When it was finished, there was a terrible silence, and into that silence bits of twisted metal, shards of glass, and plastic began to pelt against EnTa-7 and scatter across the dusty ground all around her. The sky rained debris, as if in slow motion. No pieces larger than a pebble reached her, but she could hear the drone's metal casing pinging with the tiny impacts for what seemed like several long minutes.

Tanni realized then that she had stopped running. *The recycler!* She turned toward the *RapUnsEl* and saw the twisted wreckage on the ground near the remains of the base station, its steel girders thrust into the air like the ribs of a partially consumed carrion, the innards scattered carelessly around a shallow crater.

"My god…" she heard Weaver whisper in her ear, then, "I'm going to try to raise the passengers on the comm." And he clicked off. The agents on the *RapUnsEl* were his colleagues, maybe his friends. Tanni felt a wave of nausea roll over her as she considered what he must be feeling. He had sent those people down here. He had sent them here for her. For Sam.

She sped toward the wreck as a few tiny bits of plastic continued to rain down around her. As she picked up speed, she noticed the skyhook: a tiny line in the darkening sky, which still ran straight up into the clouds, but which no longer reached the ground. A small ripple in the line, like a flick in a jump rope, disappeared into the cover of the clouds. Would she feel that when it reached Venusberg? How long would it take to travel the whole line?

Fires dotted the wreckage of the *RapUnsEl* and the nearby buildings, though with little oxygen in the air, they didn't burn brightly or for very long. Smoke mushroomed into heavy, dark plumes above the scene, obscuring the sunset in total by the time she reached the wreckage. Without much thought, she climbed EnTa-7 into the wreckage.

Inside, the air was mostly clear, with a few columns of smoke rising quickly up through holes in the thin shell of the cargo platform. Buckled and crumpled, the platform was littered with the former contents of the cargo crates. Tools, dehydrated food, furniture, building materials, the things the residents of the complex rely on being sent down from above. Things they needed to live, expand, and thrive on the surface of the hot, dusty world. As she clambered over the splintered remnants of crates and the scattered remains of their cargo, Tanni suddenly saw the waste of it. The untold amounts of money, time, and other resources spent to keep people working and living on the surface of a planet. It was astronomical, but it was necessary, wasn't it? Didn't people *need* to live on planets?

She reached the door of the passenger cabin and braced herself. The cabin walls were twisted and scorched, the cabin clearly no longer airtight. She punched the command to open the small airlock with one clawed appendage, but the door was trapped in the crushed frame. It would never open again.

She moved quickly around the outside of the cabin until she saw a rupture in the wall large enough to fit her claws into. She gripped both sides of the fissure and heaved, allowing the drone's powerful arms to rip the gap wider. The beige plastic cracked and snapped, flying away in splinters as the metal beams bent away. It was a work of only a few moments to create a gap large enough for EnTa-7 to climb through. Human forms were sprawled about the floor of the cabin, most unmoving, but some clearly struggling. The passengers had already been geared up with surface suits in preparation for debarkation, and this had saved some of their lives, but the heat in the room was intense, owing partly to a jet of fire streaming up one wall from an oxygen port.

Tanni carefully stepped over the bodies, making her way to the flames, trying not to look too closely at any of the battered, dismembered forms, knowing that it would cost her far too much. She shut off the oxygen with a flick of a claw. Nearby, a passenger, she couldn't tell if it was a Triad employee or a Sol Agent, sat against the wall, breathing heavily. He seemed to be the only person in the room with any awareness. The only person not in shock or unconscious - or dead. He turned to look at her from within his soot stained helmet, and his bloodied face was blank.

Tanni switched on her speaker. "It's okay," she told the blank face, "rescue teams will be here soon." *I hope*, she added to herself. The figure nodded, face still blank.

"I need the recycler," she said, and the man glanced across the cabin to a small green satchel lying upside down on a bench, one of the nylon shoulder straps torn free.

Agent Weaver clicked back in. "Tanni, there are three people still alive in that cabin. Two of them are my agents. They may need that recycler if rescue teams don't come soon."

Tanni hesitated, one claw gripping the remaining intact strap on the satchel. "Sam needs it," she said simply and lifted it off the bench. Her speaker was still on, and she heard her words come back to her flatly.

"Sam is safe in his dome for right now, Tanni," Weaver said, imploringly. "It's too late to try to stop the attack, and there is no way off the surface now. These people need the recycler more."

She opened the zipper of the pack with her other claw, careful not to damage the bag further. It was there, a small box and a set of hoses, basically a miniature version of the giant envi plant. She moved carefully back to the door and rolled the satchel through the opening. She looked once around the small cabin and caught the eyes of the conscious passenger. She expected to see something in that face. Sadness? Regret? Pain? Betrayal? But there was nothing, just the cold, flat, bloodied gaze.

Tanni's vision blurred as she turned to crawl back out of the room. Weaver spoke again. "Tanni, Sam is not the priority right now. We need rescue, recovery, damage assessment-" She closed the connection from her end, blinked away the tears in her eyes, and grabbed the satchel. As she picked her way back across the ruined cargo platform, she expected her connection to be cut, or her helmet to be removed at any moment, but it didn't happen. Whatever chaos was going on up in Venusberg, she was being left out of it.

She climbed back down out of the wreckage of the *RapUnsEl* and sped toward Sam. In the distance, the sun disappeared below the horizon.

As EnTa-7 sped past the mirrored glass of the labs, Tanni glanced to the side, seeing the sooty drone there, rolling smoothly, carrying a tattered green nylon satchel across its chassis like a sash. EnTa-7 was filthy, but Tanni felt even dirtier. Inside her helmet her hair was matted with sweat. Her jumpsuit was soaked through, and her own body smell filled her tiny room. Tears had dried on her face, where she couldn't wipe at them under the visor, and in her mind's eye, her face was streaked with smoke and soot, though she knew that none of it could reach her. She turned back to watch the ground ahead.

She could have stopped to clean up and regroup, she knew. It was two hours back to Sam's dome from the base station, and she could have just let EnTa-7 make the journey without her. She stayed in though. Leaving would have felt like a betrayal, and somehow, she felt that if she pulled out now, she wouldn't be able to get back in. She would be swept up into whatever must be going on in Venusberg, and Sam would be without her. She had lost connection with all of her other drones. EnTa-3 had gone dark just as she was leaving the site of the explosion, then the others vanished about an hour later. She was hungry, tired, and dirty, but Sam needed her to keep going.

She pulled around the last corner toward the Türme agricultural dome and grew immediately worried. The lights were off. In the final sunlight flowing in from the east, the dome glittered and shone, but it produced no light of its own.

Slowing, she pulled up EnTa-7's wheels and began to walk. She approached the dome cautiously, watching for any movement within. She thought she saw a figure among the trees. The exposed electric field was already down, so Tanni had no barrier to enter the area. She approached the airlock and entered the code to open it. The hiss of the lock seemed to take an eternity as she waited impatiently for the lock to open. When it finally slid aside, she slipped inside, and waited again, listening to the machines force the air pressure down to just above Earth-normal.

When, finally, the internal doors of the airlock had moved aside, she stepped slowly in. "Sam!" she called in a stage whisper. Then she noticed: the pressure suit was gone.

Oh no!

She heard a resounding clang, and her view of the empty suit-stand jarred wildly before EnTa-7 clattered loudly to the ground. Her warning lights blinked in the periphery of her vision. Several systems were out on her left side, including control of the left appendage. She pushed with her right appendage, rolling over onto her back in time to dodge the hammer end of a demolition bar as it struck the metal flooring beside her. She looked up into Thomas Türme's face as he raised the bar again with obvious effort. "It was you, wasn't it?!"

His face twisted as he raised the bar above his head. "You doomed our species!" The bar descended again, and Tanni instinctively raised her hands to block the strike. Only her right appendage came up, and the blow glanced off of the claw and struck her camera. Tanni was blinded for a moment. As white noise filled her view, the camera came back just in time to see the hammer head descending again on the other side of a branching, glittering crack in the lens. This time she reached up with her right appendage and grabbed the bar out of the air.

The impact rang and the jolt broke the bar from Türme's grip. Losing his balance, he fell forward, eyes wide with indignant shock, as he was impaled through the chest by the sharpened crow-end of the demo bar. Tanni watched stunned as the man's blood poured out over the bar and onto her claw before the view turned to static once more.

Tanni's first impulse was to shut off the helmet, her second was to vomit, but she held both at bay. She dropped the weight in her right claw off to the side, and, with difficulty, righted EnTa-7. The drone was having difficulty balancing. The damage to its side must have been severe. The room around her came into focus just for a moment. She was facing the airlock, Türme's impaled, bloodied body at her feet, then static again.

Slowly, she took a step toward the door, hearing the drone's systems struggle to cooperate. Her vision flickered, and she took another step. She had to get to Sam.

As she waited for the airlock to cycle, she reopened the channel to Agent Weaver. He must have been watching for it to open. "Tanni?" he called out immediately.

"Türme was in Sam's dome," she told him, speaking quickly. "He's dead now, but I don't know where Sam is, and EnTa-7 is badly damaged."

"Slow down, Tanni," he said in his calm, businesslike way, "I figured something was going down at the dome when I saw EnTa-3 go dark, so I sent you some reinforcements. I was hoping they'd arrive before you went charging in, but I couldn't raise you on the comm, so..."

"Reinforcements?" Suddenly Tanni's peripheral vision lit up with her remaining drones' feeds, back under her control, then another drone came up, SoTu-4, and another, SmCo-1, then another and another, then her control interface was cluttered with drones, all under her control. There must have been three dozen of them, all taken from other controllers on nearby projects.

"Your colleagues were happy to loan you the services of their drones when they learned what was going on," Weaver said.

The airlock door opened, but she didn't know it from the failing vision of EnTa-7. She saw the door open through the lenses of fifteen other drones, all waiting patiently for orders on the other side of the exposed conduit. She watched EnTa-7 stride through the door, chassis battered, burned, and bloodied; camera smashed; and left appendage dangling uselessly. "Weaver, I…"

He cut her off. "You can't worry about that now," he said flatly. "Everyone who survived the crash still lives. The rescue teams were able to reach the survivors in time, thanks to a rather large hole torn in the side of the cabin." "I'm sorry," she said.

"I told you to forget about it. You need to find Sam. How much time does he have?"

"I don't know. His suit can handle almost three hours out here, but I don't know how long it's been."

"We lost contact with EnTa-3 a little over two hours ago," Weaver pointed out.

Tanni stared as another drone rolled up to join the group that had already assembled. According to the feeds, there were still a dozen more on their way. She rolled to one of them and redirected it, pulling up a map of the colony complex to overlay her commands. The drone stopped heading toward the Türme Dome and redirected to a point on the path between the dome and the envi plant towers. She rolled to another and redirected it back to the towers themselves. She rolled through one drone after another, looking at the map and directing them to cover the area in a wide grid. The drones that had already assembled at the dome headed back out one by one along radial paths, some following the curves and bends of the edge of the complex in either direction.

Once all the drones were on the move, she began rolling among them, stopping at each for only a few seconds. Sometimes she would enter a bit of code to correct a course or redirect a camera; sometimes she would shrug into direct control and look around herself. She began rolling from drone to drone, faster and faster, until it seemed like she was controlling the entire cluster at once. She heard Agent Weaver gasp. She was more than just a drone operator, she was the admiral of a fleet. She wasn't a woman, she was the signal, amorphous and invisible, and each of the drones were one of her appendages. Her mind reached out to touch them all, their views flashing before her faster and faster, searching, seeking out Sam and his flawed suit, seeking out her beautiful dancer before he was lost to her forever. In the middle of it all, EnTa-7, the heart of this thing she had become, blind and crippled, was still holding on to the lifegiving satchel, waiting to run.

It was EnTa-1's camera that saw Sam first, bent as a man carrying a great weight, stumbling along the edge of a cubic science station, barely visible in the darkness against the concrete grey of the walls. The other nearby drones turned almost instantly toward him, and she soon saw Sam with a half-dozen eyes. Half a kilometer away, EnTa-7 turned in that direction, tossing up dust around itself as it spun.

EnTa-1 reached Sam in a few moments. "Tanni," she heard his voice weakly through the drone's microphone.

"I've got you!" she called to him, though he could not hear. His lithe body collapsed into EnTa-1 as its appendages reached out to hold him. Gently, she wrapped her arms around him as he went limp, his eyes closed, his breathing shallow. Then another drone arrived, and she wrapped those arms about him as well, and in moments she held him with six pairs of arms, but it was not enough to sustain him. He was fading.

EnTa-7 arrived with an escort of three other drones, and more were closing in on the moving cluster with Sam at its center. She lost track of which cameras went with which arms, and it didn't matter. Four claws grasped at the green satchel and tore it asunder while two others, not on the same drone, grasped the recycler and moved it into place. A flurry of action brought Sam gently to the ground and clipped each of the hoses and cables into place on the suit. The small device began to purr. Before she knew what she was doing, she was standing in the middle of a tight circle, in direct control only of EnTa-7, while the remaining drones surrounded her and Sam on all sides, as if observing a sacred ritual.

Her great, amorphous form was lost then, and Tanni felt small. She was a woman once again. She tried to look into Sam's face, but the drone was still blind, so instead she watched from nearly twenty different angles as she lifted Sam in her one good claw, his suit pressed against EnTa-7's chassis. They stayed that way for a long moment, Sam's still limp form dangling in her grasp. "Oh, Sam!" she breathed. "Please!"

As if in answer to her plea, Sam abruptly jerked in her grasp and began to breathe more deeply. Tanni's vision blurred and her face grew wet. She heard Agent Weaver let out a long breath.

Sam's eye's opened just as EnTa-7's camera came back online for another brief moment. "My charming Prince Robot..." he said with a weak smile.

Tanni laughed then, and it was as if the entire planet came off of her shoulders. "My maiden in distress..." she said, laughing.

Tanni brought her other remaining drones in closer, disconnecting herself from all of the others. She had EnTa5 and 6 form a sort of palanquin with their arms, and EnTa1 and 3 took Sam from her and gently placed him in the makeshift seat.

The party of drones began to move then, rapidly across the flat surface toward the envi plant.

"Sam," she said, "I'm sorry. It's going to be a while." "Until what?" he asked weakly.

EnTa-1's camera swung around to look at the skyhook, and Sam turned his head to look as well. "Until we dance together in Venusberg," she finished.

Last Girl

The town was surrounded by a thick wall of refuse. Most towns were. They had protected themselves against the wilderness by piling up anything they could find between the buildings at the outskirts. Often more walls divided the town inside from itself. A few places were well crafted from the bricks of fallen buildings, other places were piles of garbage, abandoned vehicles, and sometimes, the now skeletonized bodies of those who had been the most recent to die before the deadliest part of the final plague began. These were always the easiest places to get through.

The girl stepped one foot in front of the other, heel-to-toe, heel-to-toe along a concrete curb, glancing at the wall periodically, trying to find such a weak-spot. She lifted one foot for a moment, singing a quiet, indistinct song about a lovely ballerina, and savoring her newfound ability to balance on one foot without raising her arms. There were no words in her songs, only the hums and grunts that she was able to make, but the words were clear in her head.

She looked around, glancing quickly at the sky to gauge the time of day, then to the wall, where she saw what she had been looking for.

She approached the spot on the wall, where several skeletons lay upon one another, their clothing rotting off in small strips, their flesh completely removed by insects, animals, and weather over the last ten years. Dangerously sharp and rusted scrap metal was piled above them.

Warily, she reached out and pushed on the bones of the lowest body. Some ribs and a wrist cracked as she pushed, but the skeleton moved mostly in one piece, pushing others behind it, forming a crater in the wall, weakening the already tenuous section. She stopped when she heard the metal creak above her. She had pushed in almost to her shoulders anyway. Carefully, she removed her arms from the wall and stepped back. Looking around, she found a fist sized rock in the dirt. Her wiry arm flung the stone with speed against the wall just above the new crater. The wall shifted, and several pieces fell from the spot where the stone hit. She waited several moments before approaching. She found a horseshoe, a few rusted blades, a car steering wheel, and what looked like a rotted broom handle.

She picked up the steering wheel, being careful not to breathe the red dust that was settling away from the wall. She hopped back to the spot where she had thrown the stone, curled her arm around her body, and, spinning, released the wheel toward the wall. Where it hit, several more pieces of scrap fell away, then more, soon the wall was collapsing. She turned and crouched, pulling the collar of her small leather jacket up over the back of her head. The crashing behind her made an awful and painful sound. After a few moments, she stood, her thin sweater pulled up over her face to keep out the dust. The air still tasted rancid and rusty.

The wall had a V-shaped gap in it, plenty of space for a girl to climb through. She was careful not to injure herself on the sharp, rusted debris.

Walking through the streets of the town, she began singing a loud tuneless song about rusted bones. Her wordless voice reverberated off of the crumbling walls and filled the long silence of the small town. She sang and skipped and spun as she looked at each building in turn. A mile down the main drag, she found what she was looking for: A store with solid walls, windows unbroken, and locks still on the doors.

She approached the front window, still blocked by an accordion gate. The lock on the gate was completely ruined, bashed and cut almost to pieces, yet it was still closed. The window was dusty, and nearly opaque. She quickly noticed a small hole in the window.

She had seen holes like that many times. A bullet hole. She leaned in and looked through the hole with one eye. Inside, a mostly skeletonized man sat with a gun on his lap and a hole in his head.

She stepped back and took a look at the gate, then at the lock. It had the same symbols carved into it as many other unbroken locks which she had found. Perhaps those symbols meant something special.

She remembered a hardware store about a hundred yards back down the road. Its walls were broken, but perhaps some of the tools were still in good shape. As she walked, she sang a song about a tough little girl, searching for a hacksaw in a ruined city.

When she returned to the gate, she held a hacksaw fitted with the most sparkled blade that she could find, since those have always done the best job against metal in the past. She started by sawing at the lock, but after several minutes, had cut barely a millimeter through the metal, and didn't seem to be making progress. She understood why the person who killed the shop owner had been unable to break the lock. She shook out her hand, and went to work, instead, on the loop which held the lock in place. Here she made noticeable progress, and in ten minutes had the gate open.

The door behind was still locked. She tried to use the saw on this lock, but the lock plate was too close to the door, and she made very little impression. Reluctantly, she smashed in the glass door with the saw. When the dust settled, she ducked under the push-bar, and into the musty air of the grocery store.

It was not an unpleasant smell. It was sort of sweet. In the past, she'd found bodies that had been in confined spaces for years, and the odor had been unbearable. She stood before the man, leaned toward his bony face, and looked into the space where his eyes once were. She decided that he looked very sad, and that she was glad he had died quickly, with no pain. She was always glad to see that someone had died quickly, instead of- She shook the images from her head and looked again at the shop-keeper. She couldn't just leave him there. She decided to explore the rest of the store before doing anything.

Behind a small door, she found a narrow stair up to the second story. The stairs were badly damaged by termites and rot, but carefully, she was able to ascend to the landing. Glancing around, she saw that the second story was small and had only two rooms. The door to the first was standing open, it was obviously a washroom.

As always, she tried the tap, just to make sure... and as always there was nothing. She tried the second door. The bedroom: A small couch, several lamps, a dark computer console, rotting curtains, and a bed.

On the bed was another body. Beneath the women's nightgown, the bones were twisted into pretzel knots. There was a bullet hole in the front of the gown... This was the shop owner's wife or daughter or mother...

The girl looked away, but suddenly felt very sick. She screamed and clamped her fists to her temples as the images and emotions of her mother's final days came back to her in a flood of tears. Her limbs twisted in never ending agony, every moment of consciousness between fever-ridden bouts of sleep spent calling, begging for death to come, until her daughter finally decided to do as her mother said, until she finally had the courage to-

The girl turned from the room and ran back down the hall, and onto the stairs. The wood around her began to crumble away. The stairs, the walls, the banister, everything around her was turning to dust. Dust and tears.

She fell into the darkness.

She tasted death.

...the cave ... she has to leave the cave ... has to stop preening Mothers body ... has to survive ... but, Mother ... *she will never move again ... the screaming is done ... good ... good ...*

The dust in her mouth tasted like the smell of death. Something made it painful to open her eyes. She forced them open, but it was too dark to see. Her whole body was sore. She tried to move her arms. They were stuck. After a moment of panic, she realized that she was lying face-down on top of her wrists. She rolled, and then lay still, waiting for feeling to return to her wrists and hands. Several minutes passed as she bore the pain of renewed circulation.

Finally, she took stock of her surroundings. There was very little light, but she could tell that she was under what used to be a staircase. It had crumbled beneath her as she ran. *From what?* She shouldn't think about it right away. Maybe later.

She rolled back over onto her hands and knees, and felt out her immediate surroundings: A broom, a bucket, several boxes, various tools on a small shelf... She was in a closet. She suddenly felt very lucky to have only lost feeling in her hands. If she had landed a little bit to either side, she might have been seriously injured by this broom or this cabinet or this glass bottle... Feeling around some more, she found the door to the closet, and turned the knob, falling out onto the tiled floor of the shop.

There was a little more light here, coming from the moon, by way of the mostly translucent front window. She was behind the register counter. She could see rows of receipt paper on one shelf, along with other various supplies.

Slowly, painfully, she stood. With a little searching, she found a small washroom. She tried the faucet. Nothing. She looked in the mirror. Even in the low light, she could see that she was totally covered in dust and dirt. On her eyes and cheeks, the dust had crusted like dried mud. Images began to return to her:

The upstairs bathroom had a mirror much like this one. Then, down the hallway, in the bedroom... *No*... She shook the image from her head before it could fully surface. She concentrated on her own reflection. She needed water. She was dirty and thirsty.

She found some water bottles, and some rubbing alcohol in the shop, and returned to the washroom to wash herself. She used the alcohol on the cuts and scrapes, when she found them under the dust, just like her sister taught her to do, before the crazies came to the house and took her away.

When she was finished, the sun was beginning to rise, and she decided to start making this place into her home for the winter. Maybe longer if she could find enough supplies, but she didn't think she would.

As a first step, she finished looking around. In the back of the store, she found palettes of plastic tasting water, stacks of canned goods, some of them with pictures of cats and dogs on them, and another door, a heavy metal one with a big lock. She decided right away that she would spend the time to block up the front door and use this one exclusively.

She returned to the hardware store for a shovel and started digging in a patch of dirt near the back-door. She spent most of that day digging, and in the evening, she carefully carried the shopkeeper's body, and his chair, out to the grave. It was dark when she placed the marker stone over the loose dirt.

The next day, she decided to get some clothes. Her clothes were dirty, and since new clothes were free, it made more sense to get new ones than to waste water on cleaning the dust off of the old ones.

She walked around the shops until she found one that looked like what she wanted. When she went inside, she found that the store, as usual, had been split down the middle, with practical clothes on one side, and impractical, easily torn clothes on the other side. She walked back through the store, past the mostly empty racks of adult-sized clothes, to the mostly full racks of child-sized clothes. The smaller clothes were almost always still around.

She knew that someday soon she would need those bigger clothes, and she would probably have to visit people's homes to find them. She dreaded that day. There were always so many bodies in the parts of town where the houses were. She was also noticing that it was getting more difficult to fit snuggly into the practical clothes as she got older. Although there were a few pieces on the impractical side that fit, and seemed functional, so this was where most of her clothes came from on this trip.

She spent the entire day looking through the stock. She returned to her new home at nightfall, pushing a wheeled cart filled with clothing and the few blankets and pillows that the looters had missed. Everything was a little dusty, but nothing a good shake didn't help, and not nearly as bad as her old clothes, which were not just dusty, but also stained by blood and urine.

At first, she didn't recognize the sound. She sat up from her bed-roll and listened. Grinding and gurgling from far away. The growling of a sick dog.

In a flash of memory, the sound was clear. The crazies had made that sound the night they came to her house.

It was louder, closer, and mixed with the hoots and hollers that always accompanied the crazies. Father had kept the family inside since the crazies started murdering people on the street. Mostly, people who stayed in their homes were safe.

This time, however, they stopped. One of them broke a window. Another kicked in the door. Gunshots. Mother screamed as Father fell. Sister was slumped across the back of a motorcycle, and they were gone. It was over in seconds, and only she and Mother were left, and Mother couldn't live in the house anymore.

The girl sprang up, and ran toward her pack, knocking over a tall stack of emptied cans with cat's faces on them, which she'd been building up over the last couple weeks. She paused a moment, thinking to rebuild it, but decided that it could wait.

At the bottom of her pack, she found what she was looking for, a rifle scope, and rushed out the heavy door. She sprang past the small grave marker and leaped onto the ladder on the wall of the building.

When she reached the top, she listened again for the sound. The reverberations across the town made it too difficult to figure the direction, but it had to be close. She raised the scope to her eye and searched the streets.

A half-mile away, on the other side of a collapsed shopping center, she saw it: A dirty, black motorcycle. Just one, and just one rider. It was driving away from the hole the girl had made in the wall, now cleared enough to let the bike through.

She watched the bike cross the town, slowly, the rider looking left and right at the buildings, until it came to a stop in front of a convenience store only a street away. The rider dismounted. Looked around and took the helmet off.

Long, auburn hair, sharp features. *Sister!*

The girl dropped the scope and clamored down the ladder, falling the last few feet, and twisting her ankle against the grave marker. She hobble-ran between mostly fallen walls and steel beams to the convenience store. In moments, she was peering out from between two concrete columns at the store, and the big motorcycle. The rider emerged from the store with a small package in her hand: perhaps a peppery meat-stick. She sometimes could still find those on the floors and cabinets of the corner stores.

The woman leaned against an old gas-pump and opened the package. It wasn't Sister. She looked a bit like Sister, but she wasn't Sister. Trying to decide if she should leave her concealment, the girl shifted her weight, and knocked a chunk of concrete loose from the pillar. The sound startled the woman, and she turned to look, but the girl did not wait to meet the woman's gaze. She quickly ran back to her store, and after a few minutes, she heard the motorcycle start back up again.

She started the next day by sealing up the front of the store. As she nailed a tarp over the broken glass door, she sang a song to herself about a little girl trapping herself in a dangerous dungeon and tried to ignore the sound of the motorcycle still moving around the city. She was admiring her work, when she felt a breeze, somehow still coming through. She checked all the edges of the door, and felt nothing, then she remembered the bullet hole. She looked at it. It was surrounded by cracks, and looked very weak, but somehow, the window was still in one piece after all this time, so something was strong about it. She looked around the store until she found a wide roll of tape. Carefully, she placed a small square of it over the small hole in the window.

There was still a draft from somewhere. She wandered around the store, feeling for the draft. She was drawn toward the narrow wooden door, leading to the broken staircase. It was the source of the draft. She shuddered, not because it was chilly. Inside, the stairs were ruined; there was no way to reach the second story now. So, instead of seeing what was open upstairs, she stuffed bits of cloth into the seams and nailed the door closed. Then, she did the same with the closet door on the other side of the space. The air was still after that. She would be able to keep warm in here for the entire winter.

She started to feel a bit uncomfortable in the stillness. She realized that she was thinking about something upstairs. Something was right above her, and it would be there all winter, and she couldn't think about it. She couldn't think about it if she didn't want to end up like the crazies.

To distract herself, she climbed back up onto the roof to retrieve her forgotten scope. While she was up there, she took the opportunity to look for the woman again. The sound of the motorcycle had stopped, but she found the woman after only a few minutes of searching. She was at another corner-store with gas-pumps, and she was standing next to a hole in the ground, running a hose down into it. After a moment, she turned and let the hose drop down by her side, seeming to stare directly at the girl, so the girl dropped behind the lip of the rooftop to hide. When she peeked back over, the woman was still looking her way, and now she was waving.

It was three days before she saw the woman again. It had been getting colder than expected in the small shop, and the girl was searching the stores for something to hang in the large front window. She was hoping to find something to keep out the cold at night, but which she could move out of the way in the day, as that window was her only source of light.

The girl was skipping from shop to shop singing a wordless song about dancing with the sun and the moon when she spotted the motorcycle outside of the hardware store on the other side of the cracked four-lane street. She stopped and stared for a moment, and the woman peeked out from behind the doorway of the store, smiling when she saw the girl. The woman slowly stepped out onto the sidewalk on her side of the street. The girl took a step back, bumping against the wall behind her, and dropping her pack. She was about to run, and it seemed that the woman could tell because she raised her hands in a sign of non-aggression.

The girl stood still, only watching as the woman, slowly crossed the street toward her, hands still raised. When the woman was only a few feet away, she reached a hand out to the girl. The hand was dirty, and the smile was lopsided, and the girl was suddenly reminded of her the way she had to approach small animals in the forest for food.

She turned and ran then, visualizing her own blood spilling into the grass or making pretty red clouds around the rocks of a clear stream. She ran, without looking back, all the way to her store. She slammed the heavy steel door behind her and latched it. She collapsed exhausted and crying to the floor.

She spent almost all of the next day building up the courage to go back out. In the evening, she finally crept, as quietly as she could, out of her door, and back along the street. When she got there, she was surprised to find that her pack was still there. It didn't even look like it had been touched since she dropped it.

A few days later, the girl was entertaining herself in the ruins of an old toy store. She had started by playing a hunting game, where she tried to find as many intact plush animals as she could, singing a song about bears and elephants, but when she had found an entire crate of them pinned under a fallen column, she got bored with the counting.

She spent hours searching through the boxes of electronics at the back of another store, but, as always, there was not one working toy or device. However, she had found a large box full of silver-backed devices that she thought she could decorate the walls of her store with, so she loaded them all into a rope-handled paper bag, and lugged them away from the store, dragging the sturdy bag over and under broken walls, and bits of neighboring stores. It was getting dark, and the girl was tired, so she headed directly for her home. She picked back up her song about the animals, and so didn't notice the dog.

It was feral and starved. Its fur was matted and ill maintained, and before she could react it was upon her. It leapt first at her throat, and she instinctively swung the bag from the electronics shop, striking the dog away, and breaking the bag. Small boxes scattered around the street, some of them flying open, so that their mirrored cargo scuffed and scrapped against the pavement.

The dog was back in an instant and had clamped down on her ankle. The girl collapsed, howling in pain, and tried to pull away. This only caused the dog's grip to tighten. The girl struggled to draw her dagger from its sheath at her belt. The dog was shaking her, and that combined with the fear of him was making it difficult to unsnap the clasp, and grip the handle, but as soon as she had it free, she stabbed and buried the knife into the dog's coarse neck.

It let go then and thrashed on the pavement for a moment before falling still. The girl grabbed her ankle with both hands and howled again with pain, then cringed and allowed herself to collapse, supine, to the pavement. She watched the clouds for a moment, silently forcing herself to ignore the pain. She needed to get back to the store and clean and bandage the wound.

She forced herself up and took a moment to gather her knife from the dog's body. Having no way to clean it, she simply held it in her hand as she limped away. Pain pounded against her ankle with every step, and several times she stumbled and fell. It was going to be a long walk home.

Before the girl had gone a block along the road, the woman turned the corner ahead, and faced her. She looked worried. She must have heard the pained howling. When the woman spotted the girl, she stopped herself short, and took in the scene. She looked from the girl's face to her knife, to the dog in the distance behind, and finally to the bloody holes in the girl's pant leg.

The woman held up one finger, and the girl watched as the woman brought a smaller, leather bag out of her pack. She searched around in this smaller bag for a minute before she brought out a small plastic card with her picture on it, and a clip on one end. The girl had seen these before in office buildings but couldn't read the words.

With her ankle in this shape, she couldn't run anyway, so she let the woman approach, holding out the badge in front of her. When she reached the girl, she motioned for her to sit down on the curb a few feet away. The girl complied, in too much pain to protest.

Once the girl was seated, the woman started unloading her small bag onto the street around her. She carefully laid out about a dozen small silver tools, along with various little bottles and rolls of gauze. The girl understood then what the woman was doing and relaxed a bit. The woman cut away the bottom half of that pant-leg, and carefully removed it to get at the bite.

The wound stung as the woman poured clear fluid over it from a plastic bottle, but it was easier to handle when someone else was doing the pouring. The girl saw that the wound was not as bad as it felt, and as she calmed down from the attack, the pain also began to fade.

When the woman was done with her work, she tried to help the girl up, but the girl refused to be helped. She didn't want help walking either, so the woman left her alone to continue on by herself. However, the girl had the feeling, the whole way back to the little store, that she was being watched.

The day of the first snowfall, the girl saw smoke rising a few streets away. She was walking the streets, singing a song about dancing snowflakes as the new snow crunched underfoot. She had bundled herself into a bright-blue snowsuit and pink rubber boots. Some years there was no snow at all, but she liked the few days when it did snow, as it was the only way that the dark world ever looked clean.

The dark billowy column was coming from a restaurant on the main street which was still mostly intact. The girl walked around the building until she found a small window, and looked in. The woman was sitting before a fire-place against one wall. She had broken apart most of the tables and chairs and stacked them against the wall for firewood. She was sitting in a large arm-chair with a book open in her lap. The inside of the restaurant, where the woman had obviously been living was much different from the girl's home in the store. The walls and floors were mostly wood and stone, rather than concrete, and the floor wasn't covered in empty cans or discarded wrappers. The girl suddenly felt a little ashamed that she never cleaned up after herself in her own place.

The girl was starting to get uncomfortably cold standing in one place, so she decided to move on. As she passed the front of the restaurant again, she heard a door open behind her. She turned to see that the woman was standing in the doorway of the restaurant, staring at her. When their eyes met, the woman motioned to the girl that she should come inside, and then walked back inside, leaving the door open behind her.

Slowly, warily, the girl padded up to the door, and felt the warmer air escaping into the cold day. She stepped over the threshold and closed the door behind her. She could see the bar area of the restaurant now and noticed that the bar was stacked high with cans of various shapes and sizes, and that a door leading into what must once have been the kitchen was covered with a blanket nailed into the wall. The motorcycle was propped in a corner next to a bedroll. She set her pack down on the floor next to the door, and sat beside it, pulling up her knees and hugging them to her chest. The woman watched from the middle of the room as the girl settled in, and then smiled once more before returning to her arm-chair and her book.

The two sat this way for some time before the girl finally removed her snow-suit. Seeing this, the woman set down her book, and walked over to the bar. She selected a can from the stacks and carried it with her back to the fireplace. After adding a few more chair-legs, and stoking the fire a bit, she opened the can, and poured the contents into a small pot which she placed over the fire.

The smell of broth slowly filled the cozy room over the next few minutes, and when the woman finally removed the pot from the fire, the girl's mouth was watering. The woman produced two bowls from behind the bar and set them out on a table which had been left whole in the middle of the room. She set two places, complete with placemats and flatware, and then filled the bowls from the pot. She sat at one of the places, looked at the girl, and waited patiently.

Staring at the woman the whole time, the girl moved slowly over to the table, at sat at the other place. The woman began to eat then, and the girl joined her, slurping hungrily at the soup.

When the meal was done, the girl bundled herself back up and left the small restaurant for her own home, singing a song of warn soup on the way back.

The snow melted the next day, and the next few weeks were a bit warmer again. The next time it snowed, the girl returned to the restaurant, and received the same welcome, and a similar meal. Then she started visiting almost every day, looking forward to the hot meal, and the silent company of the woman. A few times she fell asleep in the woman's big comfortable arm-chair, and she would wake in the morning with a blanket over her. After the third time this happened, the woman added a second bedroll to the floor.

As winter deepened, it became more obvious that this winter would be a very cold one, perhaps the coldest that the girl had ever had to live through. She spent more and more time in the warm restaurant. The woman showed her how to tend the fire and convinced her to stop eating from the cans with the cats on them, even though those were once the girl's favorite.

On a particularly cold night, the coldest yet, the fire wasn't helping heat the small building, and both the girl and the woman were chattering their teeth and shivering violently in their bedrolls. The girl felt like she was so cold that she might die. She had seen animals die that way many times. Small cats or squirrels lying on a side-walk or under a ruined car, they look like they are sleeping, but they're frozen solid, and they never wake from that sleep.

She was picturing herself blue, and frozen stiff when she felt that another body was climbing into the bedroll with her. She wanted to fight and run, but she was too cold, and so let herself be enveloped in the woman's embrace. She too was cold, but where they touched it soon became warm, and as the cold melted slowly away, so did the girl's fear, and though she slept only fitfully, she was relieved in the morning, when the sun came up, and she was not frozen.

The next cold night, the girl went to the woman's bedroll, and placed herself into the woman's arms, who held her gently while they slept.

Mother was moaning in her sleep again. Soon it would come to screams. The girl and her mother had been in this dank, cold cave for two years. Mother had refused at first to go back to where there were any houses, where there were crazies, but now when they had seen no one else alive for three months, and returning to the houses would be easy, she was unable to move on her own any more. The girl had to find food for the both of them, and for the last few days, mother couldn't even feed herself, and even when fed could barely keep it in her mouth. The girl knew her mother was in pain, she'd been sick for months. She's been trying desperately to tell the girl, but, just like everyone else, her words had been the first thing to go when she fell ill. That was the first symptom, and no one seemed to be immune to it.

Some people she had met had simply lost their voices, and that's where it stopped for them, but most people lost their minds soon after, or worse, some were bed-ridden with inconsolable pain, their bones trying to lengthen and shorten at the same time. Most died quickly from this malady, but some, like Mother, lived on in perpetual agony.

Mother had been screaming unceasingly for a week when the girl finally understood what she needed to do. She walked over to a corner of the cave and grabbed a large rock from a pile of boulders. She took the rock over to her mother's sleeping, screaming form and raised it above her head.

The woman looked up at the girl, wide-eyed and frightened. She wasn't screaming. She wasn't making any noise at all. She was scared, but still, and patient, and confused.

The girl snapped back to the present, and lowered her arms, finding the steel pot in her hands. She dropped the horrible thing and ran horrified toward the door. She struggled with the latch, slicing her hand on the catch before flinging the door open, and running from the building. Tears froze on her face as she ran down the street, away from the memories; away from her mother's twisted, murdered corpse, just as she had done that night, years ago, searching for anyone anything to comfort her, to tell her it was okay, knowing that no one would ever tell her anything again.

She found no one out in the cold. It had snowed again, and she was bare-footed, and slightly dressed, running and slipping through the street. Not running toward anything, but just running. When she reached the town wall, here sturdy and made mostly of bricks and steel, she finally stopped. She looked down at her feet and hands, pale, and icy. She couldn't move her fingers or toes, and the wound on her hand was icing over. Her breath was short. Then she fell and the snowy gravel of the road against her face was her last sensation.

The girl awoke in the arm-chair in front of the fire. Her hand was stinging and wrapped in a bloody cloth. Her feet were bandaged as well, and she could tell from the shape of the bandages that several toes were missing. This was more curious than frightening, and she reached out to touch the place where her smallest toe had been on her right foot.

Her hand was grabbed by the woman, unseen beside her, and the woman's other hand waggled a finger. The girl saw that the medical bag was out again on the table nearby, surrounded by the small shiny tools she had seen weeks ago on the street. The girl looked up at the woman, who smiled sadly back at her.

Spring always comes. Even after a cold, long winter like that one, spring always comes. When the days grew warmer again, the girl began to think about moving on from the town. She would spend the warmer months, as she always did, searching for her sister, although each year she felt less and less like she could ever be found.

The girl was packing her important things back into her pack, getting ready to never come back to this store, to this town. As she was placing several unopened water-bottles into her pack, she heard the motorcycle start up. She hadn't heard the motorcycle in weeks and figured that the woman had decided it was time to move on, as well. It was a nice day, and there would be no more cold days until next winter.

The girl realized then that she would miss this town, not for the store, or even for the restaurant, but for the woman who lived here with her these past two months. She would miss the warm soup, and the quiet company that the woman had brought, but she'd been on her own for four winters now, and she could be alone again without trouble. Soon, she wouldn't even miss it anymore.

After a few minutes, the motorcycle was still running, and it sounded like it was getting closer. The girl realized that the sound was coming from just outside the store. She grabbed her pack, having just finished loading it anyway, and said goodbye to the store with a pat of her hand against one wall. She went out the heavy back-door, without bothering to close it behind her, and rounded the building to see the motorcycle.

The woman was sitting astride the bike, dressed the same as she was the day the girl had first seen her. Her helmet was dented, but shiny, and the black jacket and jeans looked comfortably worn-in. The woman was holding herself in place with her feet, and when she saw the girl she lifted the visor of her helmet, and the girl could see in her eyes that she was grinning.

The girl looked the bike over, and noticed something new. Hanging from the seat behind the woman was a shiny blue helmet, slightly smaller than the one the woman was wearing. The woman reached back, and unhooked the helmet from the bike, holding it out to the girl.

The girl strode up to the offer, long-since having lost her shyness or worry about the woman's nature. She took the helmet and pulled it down over her ears without a second thought. Without really knowing how, she climbed onto the back of the bike, and hugged the woman tightly. After some adjustments of their sitting positions, they were ready to go, and as they left the city, the girl hummed along to the words in her head, a song about two best friends exploring the ruins of a lost and forgotten world.

Off Day

When the jumper appeared over the horizon, Otis was in his garden, a small red fruit in his hand. A worn reed basket hung from his other arm, with four of the fruits already in it. He stopped and stared at the thing. He had seen jumpers pass over before, but this one was headed directly for him. After a few moments he looked up to the beacon on top of the two-story house. Still smashed. Still off the grid. As the jumper touched down a few meters from his vegetable patch, blowing the dry soil up in puffs around it. He could smell the death of the soil as he looked around for more vehicles. Nothing but rocks and dust all the way to the horizon in every direction, just like every day. This clean, shiny jumper was an intruder, an invasion. It sat crouched on his sand, facing him, waiting for him to make a move, or maybe for the dust to settle around it, before it attacked. The opaque wind-screen offered up no clues, no personality, no indication of purpose. Otis glanced at his roof again. No light or faint buzz. Those had ended thirty years ago when he had climbed up on the roof and smashed the beacon with a wrench. He finally placed the plant in the basket and set the basket down. He needed to harvest the remainder of this crop before nightfall, but there was not much, and it was only noon. He had time.

By the time the door of the jumper opened, Otis had moved over to his front paved walk, and removed his hat to let the slight breeze blow over his bare scalp. He closed his eyes against the dust, and scratched at his grey, tufted beard while he listened to the jumper power down and the hydraulic hiss of the opening door. A moment passed before he heard a voice, "Otis Collier?" He found himself surprised at the sound of the voice; there was something different about it, something wrong in the timbre. He opened his eyes to see the speaker. Of course: a woman. He felt silly then. Had it really been so long since he'd heard a woman's voice that he didn't recognize one anymore?

"Mr. Collier?" She was clearly an official of some-kind. Her clothes were very similar to professional attire he'd seen as a young-man: The vest was cut tighter to her waist, and the blouse was a brighter pattern of colors, but styles hadn't changed much in thirty years. Her hair was pulled back severely, although one rust-colored lock had escaped and fallen into her face. Her expression was one of worried curiosity. He tried a smile, and it only seemed to deepen her worry. She raised her hand to the nearly invisible visor on the side of her face, and then looked around. Otis could barely make out that her eyes were flicking back and forth, as she read something on the tiny screen in front of her left eye. She spotted the beacon on the roof, and frowned, a flick of her finger indicating that she'd made some adjustment to the document appearing on her visor.

"Please," Otis's voice cracked when he spoke, not from lack of use, as he spoke to his plants every day, "Call me Otis."

Relieved, the woman pushed the stray lock behind her ear, and flashed a professional smile. "I'm Jade Oliver of the Office of Off-world Affairs." She stepped forward and extended a hand to him.

He moved to take it, but stopped himself short, "You'll excuse me, Miss Oliver, if I don't take your hand; I've been working in the garden." He gestured behind him to the half harvested crops.

She nodded, and let her hand drop to her side. Her eyes followed his gesture, and she saw the rows of stalks and leaves. There had once been a fence around the property, and the remnants of the posts could still be seen along the edges of the garden, but no one had maintained the barrier since before there were still rabbits and deer to protect the garden from, "What do you grow here?"

He looked out over his garden, as if he needed to remind himself, "Mostly Soy, of course, but I indulge myself with some strawberries and tomatoes," He gestured to the fruit in the basket on the ground next to the house, "Would you like to try one?"

She made a sour face, and for a moment Otis could see the little girl behind her features, "Too bitter for my palette, I'm afraid. Thank you for offering."

Otis shrugged. "If you didn't come all this way to try my strawberries, Miss Oliver…"

"Yes, of course," she continued to stare at the basket of fruit while she spoke. The stray lock of hair fell back into her face, "Mr. Collier… Otis, do you know what tomorrow is?"

He laughed and put his hat back on. "Of course I know, miss. It's marked out in red on my calendar. I'd wager I've been preparing for Off Day since before you were born."

He expected this to annoy her - he had unconsciously calculated it to do so, but she only continued to stare at the basket. "So, you're ready to go then?"

"I'm ready, Miss Oliver, but not to go anywhere. I've lived in this house all my life, as did my father and grandfather. I'm not leaving this place."

"I've been ordered to take you back to the office in my jumper," she said gesturing to the small craft behind her, "no one is allowed to stay. The last ship leaves in the morning, and the last of the envi plants will be shut down. Nothing will remain living on this planet for long after."

She finally turned away from the basket of strawberries to look at Otis considering, almost as if she hadn't seen him before now. Then, she took a lecturing tone, "The directives are clear: The colony must move to an orbital station. Living on a planet which cannot naturally support us is archaic, almost anachronistic." Otis let her speak without interruption, though he had heard it all before. He liked listening to her voice. It wasn't sweet or pretty, but it wasn't his own voice either, and as much as he hated to admit it, it was nice to hear someone else's voice. After a few moments Otis realized that he wasn't even listening to her words anymore, just her voice.

"This is the future," she was saying when he turned back in. "No more need to waste resources on terraforming, air cleaning, escape velocities, communicating through atmosphere…" she trailed of when she noticed him smiling at her.

"You're obviously very passionate about this," he said.

"It's good to have a job that you can be proud of."

"Yes, well… today is my last day. There won't be any need for the OWA once the entire population is on the orbital base."

"I'm sorry to hear that."

"It's progress."

"So it is."

They both looked back to the garden. Otis took a step over to a wooden bench, and sat, removing his hat again, and scratching his beard. Another breeze blew across the dusty plains, nothing but rocks and dirt for miles and miles around his small patch of green. Twenty years ago, before the first of the envi plants had been shut down, the whole plain was grass and trees. A hundred years before that, before the first of the envi plants had been switched on, before the colonists had arrived, and his great grandfather had staked this plot of land, it had all been porous pink rock. Someday, it would be porous and pink again. Rocks aren't sentimental for the past.

"How did you find me?"

"Your Off Day beacon, of course." she said, "While it seems that the light and transmitter have been damaged, it still has a passive ID chip. We wouldn't want to accidentally miss someone at the end." She smiled disarmingly.

For a few moments he stared up at the roof in shock, then he smiled back at Jade, and finally, he couldn't help but laugh. "For thirty years, I thought that no one was coming to see me because I... because my beacon was damaged." he managed to get out between the hoarse guffaws of a person unpracticed at laughter, "and now I find that it's just that no one had any reason to see me anyway." He laughed for a few more moments, and then let it die abruptly, and with a deep sigh.

She frowned, not seeing the humor. "We would have been out sooner, if your beacon had been fully functional. We've been checking on the progress of such outskirted habitations for months, ensuring that everyone was packing up, and getting ready in plenty of time. We would have missed you entirely if I had not suggested that we do a final high-powered scan for the passive IDs."

"And when they found one, they sent _you_ to see if I was still here."

"Yes."

"Well, you found me," he said, "and I apologize that you've wasted your time."

"Is there no one in the main colony whom you wish to see?"

"Nah," he said, without thinking, "I've never had much need for friends, and I found out long ago that I'm not a family man."

For a moment, she looked as if she wanted to say something, but thought better of it. Instead, she turned again to look at the garden, then up at the pinkish mountains in the distance. Otis wondered if in all her life she had ever truly been outside. He had heard stories of the main colony, and when his father had told of the metal city, built mostly from the remains of the colony ship, he had always sounded a bit sad, and Otis felt sorry for all those people made to live in a can, while he got to live out here in the beautiful world.

If the initial orders had been followed since he read them so long ago, most of the citizens should be up in the citystation by now. They would only need one. The colony hadn't grown much since the early days, and the directives ordered a suspension of fertility programs until the citystation was ready. Still, Otis had seen at least two ships go up every day for the last two months.

As if reading his thoughts, a faint pop sounded from the northwest, from the direction of the main colony. Otis looked over his shoulder at the tiny upside down candle in the distant sky which had, for some years been his only evidence that he was not the only man on the whole planet. When he looked back, he saw Jade had also turned around, and was looking over his head at the ship, undisguised excitement on her face. "I've never seen the ships launch from this distance," she said, "It looks so... slow." She watched it until it disappeared into the sky beyond view, then lowered her eyes to Otis. He had been staring at her slack-jawed, and he composed himself quickly, putting his hat on so it blocked his eyes from hers.

"I'm sorry," he said, "for a moment you looked just like... like someone else."

Jade took the few steps to the bench and sat beside him. Her smell was too sweet, and it made Otis want to turn away from her, but instead he turned and peeked out at her from under the straw brim. She gave him a sad smile, "You have to come with me, Otis," she said, "Is there anything you want to get from the house first?"

He pushed himself up from the bench then, and turned to look down at the woman, who pushed the stray lock out of her face once more as she watched his slow deliberate movements. "Would you like to come in, Miss Oliver?" he asked, "You're probably thirsty, and there is something in the house I want you to see." He walked over to where he had laid his basket on the dirt, picked it up and walked around to the front door. Jade was still sitting at the bench, so he motioned for her to follow before stepping inside.

The house was all one floor with cooking surfaces and tools at one end, and tables and chairs at the other. All of the surfaces were kept meticulously clean. The steel of the kitchen, and the simulated wood dining table were both clean and polished. The plastic floors were swept clean.

Several books, none of them fiction, were stacked neatly on a small shelf over a reading chair in one corner. A narrow staircase ran up the back wall to the second floor, and underneath it sat a shining net-node in a tiny alcove. Otis hung his hat on a small hook near the door and set his basket on one of the counters next to a dehydrator which was currently filled with sliced tomatoes. The door opened and Jade came into the dim room, pausing at the threshold to allow her eyes to adjust while Otis washed his hands at the sink.

"Make yourself at home, Miss Oliver," Otis started, "I'm afraid I haven't much to offer guests right now. Would you like a glass of water or a tomato juice?"

"No, thank you," she glanced around the room. Her gaze fell momentarily on the net-node, and she raised an eyebrow quizzically.

"Oh, I never use that thing, of course," he said, "but that's no reason not to take care of it. Do you need to jack in?"

She stared at it for a moment longer and shook her head. She raised one hand to tap her visor with one fingernail, dislodging the lock of hair once more. "I'm always connected," she said.

"We had those in my day, as well, but I'd wager you've never looked at the net the way we would... I've got some NeWorld pills stashed somewhere, but they may be expired if such things do expire," he explained while opening a drawer and moving some things around, "Aha!" He drew out a small, faded plastic box with a decades old version of the NeWorld logo on it.

"Where did you get these?" she asked.

"You look surprised," he said, "I was once a NeWorld user, but after my wife passed, there was no one left to jack in with, and the games aren't as much fun alone."

"No, I guess not, I'm sorry," she said somberly, then "What happened… to your wife"

Otis looked at her carefully, trying to read her eyes. They were flat, and unconnected, but at the same-time they held a certain depth that he couldn't place. He watched as she put her hair back into place again, just like her, just like his wife had done over and over, every day. In the half-light of his kitchen, he could almost believe that he was standing right across from her, but did this girl really look like her, or had it just been so long?...

66

"My wife was pregnant with our first child when she fell ill. Illness is not usually trouble, even all the way out here, but this was strange and dire. I tried to take her into the city, but she didn't make it through the journey, it was too difficult for her." He stammered a moment, "If we had had a nice jumper like yours, or if we had been just a bit closer to the city…"

"…or if they had sent someone out to you?" she finished for him.

He gave her a sad smile, "None of the surgeons would come out this far." he said, "This was right about the time of the proclamation from Earth."

"I'm sorry," she said again, obviously not used to such situations.

He held the small box out to her, "You sure you don't want to jack-in, I don't mind."

"No, thank you," she said, "You had something to show me…"

"Yes, of course," he said, "I'm sure you're busy." He dropped the small box of hallucinogenic pills back into the drawer and closed it.

"Actually, coming out here is my last assignment as an OWA officer," she said over her shoulder as she wondered across the kitchen, past the net-node, and over to the reading chair, "I just need to be on the rocket in the morning and…" her voice trailed off as she read the titles of the books on the shelf, "These are all about gardening."

"Yes. Are you interested in gardening?"

"Erm… no, but I've never seen books that weren't classic collectables," she said, "my father has one shelf of books like this, which he never touches, they're all the ancient classical writers: Shakespeare, Poe, Asimov, you know. These books aren't like that, they have really been used," she reached out and touched the spine of one book, running her finger over an embossed title, "Are they paper?"

He laughed then, "How old do you think I am?"

She looked sheepish, "Sorry, I've just always heard about how wood used to be so common that they made books out of it."

"My grandfather once told me the same, but I've never seen it myself," he said, "He smuggled one paper book with him from Earth when he was drafted into the colonization program, but he sold it long ago, when he realized what it was worth out here."

"He must have had a lot of stories to tell."

"Yes, he did," he said, "What about your family?"

"What?"

"Well, was your great grandfather a conscript or a volunteer?"

"A volunteer," she said, "He piloted one of the sleeper ships."

"Is that still a fine point back in the city?"

"That my great grandfather was a pilot?"

"That he was a volunteer."

"No," she said. Then, "Well, sometimes my parents' generation still makes a comment about some families being from volunteer stock, and others from conscript stock, but my generation doesn't really see it that way anymore. The families are all so mixed up now it's too difficult to tell anyway."

"That's good to hear," he said.

"You see," she said smiling again, "the city's not so bad as it was, you would do fine there, I'm sure of it, even though we'll all be up in the station."

"Here," he said, as if he hadn't heard her, "let me show you this." He had stepped over to a small rug in the living room, and lifted it aside, revealing a ring in the floor, which he tugged to reveal a spiral stairwell, leading down into the darkness.

He started to descend into the floor, "Just let me go first, so I can get the lights for us."

Jade took a few steps closer and looked down into the darkness. Otis fumbled for a moment, groping for the panel that would activate the lights and brighten the short hallway. "What is all this?", Jade asked from above, once the light was on.

Otis looked up at her. He paused for a moment, seeing her face lit from below, and framed in the relative darkness of his house above. He shook himself internally. "My father passed away a few years before my wife," he explained as she began to descend the stairs, "he had some investments left over, so I sold them all, and used the funds to have this place installed after my... after the proclamation," He took a step through a large, bulkhead door while he spoke. The stainless steel room beyond was lined with shelves on both sides, a bed and a small counter with a sink were installed in the back, next to a small door that could only be a bathroom. "It's not as big as the house upstairs, but it's big enough, and as you can see, it's stocked with all the things one needs for a long stay."

He gestured around the room at each of the things in turn, "plenty of dried food, a water recycler, bed and bath facilities, a shelf for my books, and a CO2 scrubber and oxygen tanks in the ceiling, in case the few live plants I bring with me aren't enough. A man could live fifteen years in this room, which I daresay is more time than I have left to me.

"So, you see, Miss Oliver? I'm prepared for Off Day. When the last envi plant shuts down, and the atmosphere begins to float off into space, I'll be safe and sound in here."

She stared up and down the shelves at thousands of plastic-wrapped packages, "you dried all this yourself?" she asked, "from the garden outside?"

"I did," he said, "I had plenty of warning, so it really wasn't much work at all."

"But why?" she asked, an expression of clear confusion on her face, "Why not just come with us to the new station?"

"This is my home Miss Oliver," he said, "I've lived in this house since the day I was born, and it's part of me now. I would never leave this place. Not for anything."

"But this is not your home, it's just a room, and the accommodations are smaller than you would have on the city-station."

Otis considered this for a moment, "Perhaps that's true, but this is _my_ place. I'm the captain here, and all the rules and regulations are my own." He picked up a bundle of dried tomatoes and glanced around the room.

"That's what this is all about?" the way she said it didn't sound like a question, "You don't like authority?"

"No, that's not it, really," he started, "maybe it was once, but the reason for all of this has changed so much over the years. Originally, it was a political statement. Now, I don't know... I guess I'm just used to the idea of spending the rest of my life alone in this box. I've put thirty years of work into preparing this room for Off Day. It would be a shame to let all that go to waste."

"Political?" she mused. "You don't agree with the directive?"

"The directive was fine. Made sense even," He looked down at the bundle still in his hand, "but we should have been let to come to those conclusions on our own. We don't need Earth's directives."

"Earth is the seat of all governments."

"And why is that, do you think? Is it because we cannot govern ourselves?"

"Well, I don't really…"

"You haven't really thought about it." he said, showing a spark of the passion these conversations once brought out in his own father. "Earth always has been the authority, and it will be forever if we let it, but we don't need them." He slammed the package back on its shelf, almost breaking it. For a moment Jade simply stared at him, clearly at a loss. Otis realized then that his face had twisted with anger, and he had been nearly shouting at the girl. She must think his solitary life has left him a bit mad, and perhaps she would be right.

She glanced nervously at the door of the room and shrank toward the door. He finally took control of himself and allowed his face to soften. He tried to smile again, but knew how unpracticed it must look "I'm sorry, Miss Oliver." he said, his voice returning to the soft crackle that it had been outside. "I suppose I haven't moved past these ideas as much as I thought I had. It's been so long since I really thought about the politics…" he let his statement trail off, shaking his head.

Jade stood, tucked the stray lock of hair behind her ear, and walked out of the room. "I think I will take that glass of water now," she said simply as she walked up the stairs and back into the house above.

Alone in the small room, Otis turned to the small mirror above the sink, and tried his smile on himself. It was overly toothy and did look a bit mad. He sighed, and turned to follow Jade, grabbing one of the tomato packages on the way. When back up in the house, he saw that she had placed herself on a stool close to the door and was pointedly not looking at him. He turned and closed the floor panel with one hand, holding the plastic package in the other.

He walked back into the kitchen and set the package on the counter next to the basket. He could feel her silently watching him as he pulled a glass from a cupboard, and filled it from the tap. He turned and placed the glass before her on the counter.

"Thank you," she said, and took a sip.

"Miss Oliver, I -"

"I don't believe you." She said, cutting him off.

"What?" Otis was surprised. What didn't she believe?

"You say that you want to live in that tiny little hole for the rest of your life, but I don't believe you."

"Then why -"

"I'm sure you meant to when you first built it, in your grief, and your overblown political righteousness, you meant to be making a place for yourself to live," she said, "but that's not what that is. That's a tomb, not a shelter. You know that you would have a better life, be happier, on the station." "I'm happy here."

"You're a martyr here, Otis," she pushed the lock of hair out of her face, which was now fierce and more angular than he had noticed before, not angry, but fervent. "This isn't a solution. It's not even a statement, it's a penance. You think you don't deserve to live in the stars. Why?"

"The- The Earth has no right to- to-"

"What did you do?" she demanded

"I killed her," he said, softly, resignedly. Then, seeing her shocked expression, "I didn't murder her, but I might as well have. She was fragile, and I made her stay out here with me and my damn garden. She wanted to live in the city, but I wouldn't have it. That's what killed her."

Jade was silent then, once again out of her element, her streak of youthful wisdom brought to a sudden close. She took a long sip of the water, seeming to be thinking about how to respond.

"You're not going to even use that room, are you?"

The question surprised him. In years he hadn't given it as much as a single consideration. He was preparing to live in the shelter after Off-day. That had become his whole existence, but now?

"Look," she was saying, softly, "You can come back with me right now. Come to the city, and ride with me up to the new station. I'll make sure you get nice quarters, and even get you a job in a hydroponics lab..."

"It's too late for me now," he said glancing sadly over at the little carpet in the floor of his living room, "It's just too late."

She sighed, "Nothing's ever too late."

"That's an expression for young people, Miss Oliver." She looked away, "I suppose it is." "What will you do?" he asked.

She reached up and pushed a button on her visor." I should call in to the director, have him send some police to arrest you," she said, "The directive is clear. There are no exceptions…"

She sighed again, and turned toward the door, reaching for the handle. When he called out to her, she stopped and turned. Perhaps she thought she'd changed his mind; She raised an eyebrow when she saw that he was simply holding out the plastic package of dried tomatoes. He tried another smile, with fewer teeth this time, he hoped.

She looked at the packet for a moment before reaching out to accept it. She thanked him almost silently and held the bundle against her vest with one hand. She nodded to him without smiling back and turned again to leave.

"What will you tell them?" he asked.

She paused with her hand on the door's lever, not turning around, the stray lock of hair falling into her face. "No one was here when I arrived. All the residents of this household died many years ago." She pushed the lever down and stepped out into the sunlight.

Otis leaned back against the counter and let the door slam closed behind her. He closed his eyes and ran his hands over his bald pate. Listening for a moment, he heard the hydraulic door of the jumper, then the whine of the small jets. He put his hat back on and pushed the door open. He wanted to finish harvesting those strawberries before nightfall.

The Admiral

"This is a war, Mr. Chairman!" Admiral Tria had never raised her voice to the leader of the Sol Council before. Chairman Lee was stunned. He had only spoken directly with Tria on five occasions, and they had never been at odds about an important issue. He hardly knew how to react. The passion and frustration on her face reminded him of the fierce determination that was evident in holos of her from earlier in her career, which he presently had sitting on his desk. He looked down at them as an excuse to look away and compose himself. The holo on top was taken when she was transferred to an exploratory vessel for disciplinary reasons. She was twenty-five and appeared delicate. Her cadet ID, from several years earlier, lay just beneath that one. The Chairman had heard stories that the soldier who snapped that holo had laughed at her, told her that she would wash out in a few days. The Chairman smiled.

Feeling more composed, he looked back up at the Admiral's face on the screen. He let his smile show through to her, which only served to frustrate her further. He could tell that she had been about to expand on her previous comment, or maybe rehash her earlier explanations, but now she only raised a white eyebrow inquisitively, waiting for him to speak. The Chairman's office was quiet. As he stood, he heard the tiny mechanical purr of the camera following his moves. He stepped around to the front of his desk and leaned back against it with a sigh. His arms folded.

"No, Admiral Tria," he said simply, "this is not a war."

"But, Chairman-"

"This discussion is over," The Chairman interrupted, "Thank you for your input." He pushed the button on the desk behind him, cutting the connection. The screen grew dark, but the chairman could still see the face of the admiral, and he could still hear her words. After a moment, he pushed the button again. The face of his personal assistant appeared on the screen.

"What can I do for you Mr. Chairman?" the young man asked stoically.

"I want a conference call with the Secretary of Defense and the Secretary of Xenological Relations."

The young man looked confused for a moment, then flustered. He stuttered, "Wh-What should I tell them is the r-reason for the call?"

"Don't."

"Yes, Mr. Chairman. R-right way, Sir."

The screen went black again. Chairman Lee strolled back around his desk, and settled into his chair, which conformed around him as he sat.

"I hope you're wrong, Admiral" He said aloud to the empty room.

Kate Tria was eighteen years old, finally. Her family and friends sang her a song. As the song played, she looked around at their faces. The song made a hollow sound in her ears, and she looked through them. She looked through her father and mother. She looked through her brothers. She looked right through her girlfriend into the sky beyond. She saw the arc of the hoop that was the spincity, glowing in the night sky. She looked out into the vacuum of space and remembered the love for the stars she had always had as a girl. In a flash, she realized that it was this love which should guide her. From one moment to the next all worry of where she was going to be after her mandatory schooling was finished was wiped away. She was going to fly between the stars. Nothing could stand in her way

Her family looked back with the same look of love and adoration that she was giving the stars. The song ended, and Kate leaned in toward the cake. With her next breath, she decided that her wish would come true. She would grasp the inky emptiness of space, and rule it

In the next few moments, she refocused on the people around her. None of them had any idea that she wanted to fly, but all of them would be happy for her; All of them but one. She looked at her girlfriend. Kate and Griz had been best friends since childhood, but their romance was still fresh and exciting, and it would not survive this decision. For a moment, her eyes stopped smiling with the rest of her face. The young woman noticed. She cocked her head to the side, slightly, and her look changed to one of concern. Touched by this, Kate smiled fully once more and moved a hand to hook a bit of jet black hair behind her left ear. Griz was reassured.

The candle smoke cleared, and the clapping stopped. Griz picked up the gift nearest to her on the table, "Open mine first, Katie." she said as she handed the package over to the birthday girl. Kate absently began to pull the colorful wrapping from the box. Her small, delicate looking hands stripped away the folds of red paper. The box was small and white. Neat black lettering stood out on the top in Griz's careful hand:

For Katie. Happy Birthday! -Griz.

Kate opened the small box. Inside, five parallel silver chains, sharing a single clasp, formed a delicate bracelet. She put it on right away and held her wrist up to the light. The chains sparkled.

Admiral Tria was absently running her fingers over the dull, grey chains around her wrist. There were four of them, with a gap for a fifth in the middle. The missing chain was left unrepaired intentionally. It reminded her that she was not perfect; that she sometimes made mistakes.

She thought that the Chairman would be just as appalled as she was, but her description of the events did not move him to action. If something that horrible could not impel the Sol Council, then what could?

She turned to the Ensign nearby. He had just switched off the console to the video communication unit in the wall of the council room on the SCS Europa, the flagship of the Sol Council Exploratory Fleet. The room was empty other than these two. "Ensign, do you think that I'm making a mistake?"

The Ensign looked surprised. He wasn't expecting the admiral to even look at him, much less ask him such an important question. He was just there to run the conference center, not make decisions. He hesitated for a moment, but he spoke clearly when he did speak, "Admiral, I'm hardly qualified to make a judgement about --"

"Ensign," She cut him off, "When I ask you a direct question, I expect an honest and immediate answer to the best of your ability. You were running the translation boxes during the first contact, and you were standing by the door during my entire conversation with the Chairman. In my book that makes you the second most qualified person to make judgments about the situation. What do you think?"

This time, the ensign did not hesitate, "I think the Chairman is right, Admiral. The attack could have been the result of a mistake in communications. First contact has been difficult for every new sentient race that we discover."

"It didn't seem different to you this time?"

"I'll admit, they did seem unusually aggressive."

The Admiral nodded silently and eyed the young man carefully. "You blame yourself." She stated simply

The Ensign looked shocked again, "Admiral, I..." but he was lost for words.

"You were running the equipment," she continued, "and you think it was your failure as a technician that caused the first contact mission to become a massacre."

The man lost his stance, forgetting himself, and obviously uncomfortable. He looked guiltily down at his black boots, which shifted slightly under the legs of his blue coverall.

"At attention, Ensign" The admiral barked, quickly. The man regained his composure immediately, although he looked slightly frightened, as if he feared a punishment for his behavior. "I know it won't make you believe it, but I'm confident that there was nothing that any of us could have done about the situation earlier today. There is something different about these strangers. I believe that we have met our first truly Xenophobic star-faring race."

She stood, and turned away from the young man, toward the stars in the conference room porthole. "It's not just that they attacked us: Every other race in the galaxy has always sent diplomats or explorers into first contact situations; this is the first time a race has ever sent warriors. Their biology is so different from anything we've ever seen before, like they were built for combat. Even their name for themselves: The Menace." She trailed off, "But, you were here when I said all this to the Chairman."

"I was."

"And?"

"Of course, you're right, Admiral."

The Admiral turned her head quickly in The Ensign's direction, her shoulder-length, white hair swaying around her face. She considered his expression, searching for a sign of derision or sarcasm. She found none. He had simply been making an observation; perhaps an unqualified one, but not a dishonest one. She nodded simply and dismissed him with a wave of her hand.

Kate Tria sat in the plush green and purple office. She sat in one of four chairs that spanned one wall. Across from her, sitting behind a purple desk, was a small woman dressed in a conservative black and red suit. Her desk was almost bare. There wasn't even a terminal on the slick, dark surface, only a leather blotter, a small stack of papers, and a name plate with a hole in it for storage of a single ink pen. Kate looked at the name plate for the twentieth time. Her gaze was continually drawn to the plate, being the only permanent fixture in the room which appeared metallic. It was silver. It said 'Dr. Besley' in large serif-strewn letters, then 'ship psychologist' in smaller letters near the bottom.

"I asked you a question, Ensign Tria."

Kate looked up as if seeing Dr. Besley for the first time, though she'd already been speaking with her for several minutes. Kate looked through the doctor at the purple wall behind her, and the doctor regarded her with a look that very much resembled concern. When Kate could refocus her eyes, she spoke, "What was the question?"

The Doctor's frown deepened, "Why did you attack Captain Gethen?"

Kate dropped her head into her hands. Her arms were still sore, and she could feel scrapes on her face, where she must have fallen against the floor of the bridge. She could also feel the sedatives still flowing through her body. She looked back up and shook her head to clear it, "Gethen goosed me."

Doctor Besley looked confused, so Kate tried to clarify, "He grabbed my bottom." She paused for a moment, waiting for the doctor's reaction before clarifying further, "...in front of the whole flight crew."

The doctor seemed to be considering this for a moment, "That was cause to physically assault him?"

"He physically assaulted me," The tranquilizer was wearing off, and Kate was feeling a bit more lucid now that she had something to say, "I was defending myself."

The doctor paused, as if thinking. The only sound in the room: the repeated tap of her pen against the desk. After a moment, she stopped herself from the nervous habit and said, "Ensign, there is a whole department of the military designed specifically to deal with threats of that nature, you should have-"

"No," Kate cut her off, "That never works. I've tried, and they never do anything. Besides, I had to show the rest of the flight crew that I was not okay with it, that I was not to be treated that way."

Doctor Wesley adopted a look of understanding, "I know how you feel, Ensign, but it doesn't change the fact that you physically assaulted the Captain of your ship." The doctor watched as Kate placed her head back in her hands. "By policy you should be discharged immediately," she sighed, "but you must be a damn good pilot, because you've just been reassigned. The Captain demanded you off of his ship, which is his right, but Admiral Cook has placed you under another captain's command."

Kate looked up at the doctor, relief spreading across her face. She should have punched the captain months ago. "Where am I going?" she asked.

The doctor looked down at the sheet of paper lying on top of the stack on her desk. "You're headed to the Mercury."

Kate grinned. The SCS Mercury was an exploring vessel, top level priority, top level technology... A dream assignment.

"When do I leave?" Kate was having trouble containing her enthusiasm.

The doctor sighed again. "You'll leave this ship at the next port, and transfer from there. You are to be confined to your quarters until that time. Commander Kline will give you the details later. That's all I know."

"Thank you, Doctor Besley" Kate stood up to leave, her head completely clear.

"Don't thank me," said the doctor with yet another sigh, "If it were up to me, you would have been sent home"

Kate frowned at this before turning and stepping out of the office into the corridor. Once outside, with the door sealed behind her, she performed a small version of her personal victory dance, barely able to contain a shout of excitement that was welling up inside of her.

The Admiral tossed in her sleep, images of the massacre still floating around in her head, making her sleep fitful and draining, rather than restive. She awoke, startled. She sat up in bed and rubbed her stiff neck. The cuff of her pajama bottoms brushed the thin carpeting as her feet landed on the ground beside her bunk. Her free hand moved to the terminal at her bedside and keyed up the replay of the events of the previous day for what felt like the thousandth time. She didn't quite know what she was looking for. Perhaps some sign of what she could have done differently, perhaps some proof that she could have done nothing.

She watched as the Communications Officer moved into the frame and instructed The Ensign to set up the universal translation processor. It was a small beige box, which The Ensign was presently placing atop a tripod. The new species could be seen approaching in the distance, bright red, jagged outlines, but clearly bipedal. She watched as they drew near, their crystalline nature becoming clearer. The ensign flipped on the device, carefully watching the readout on the display, rather than watching the newcomers. For the hundredth time, she wondered how it was possible for him not to stare at a never before seen species of sentient starfarers.

The Admiral was distracted by an obtrusive beep, and a blinking light in the corner of the console display housing. She touched the light, and the face of the ship's captain appeared on the screen. He looked troubled.

"Admiral?" he said simply as a way of asking to speak.

"Go ahead, Captain"

"Some of their ships seem to have followed us. We're still at quite a distance, but they are faster, and will catch us in about Thirty-five minutes."

"Thank you, Captain. I'll be on the bridge shortly."

"Yes, Admiral." He said and closed the link.

The terminal screen switched back to the playback of the day before just in time for the communications officer to collapse in a bloody heap. Not having braced herself for it this time, The Admiral cringed and squeezed her eyes shut. Recovering, she watched the grizzly recording for another few moments before keying in the command to shut off the display.

The bridge was surprisingly calm when she arrived. A few members of the bridge crew were busy analyzing data, or testing communication channels, but most of them were just staring at the small view screen, waiting for something to happen.

The Captain approached to give her the details. "We're still about 25 minutes ahead of them at these speeds." He began, "We haven't gotten any indication as to their intent, but we believe that their ships are better armored and better armed than ours."

"The only other thing that we know about them is that they are unusually aggressive." The Admiral pointed out, "seems like a bad combination of information. How many of them are there?"

"Three of them broke away from the main fleet and began to follow when we left."

"So, they've matched our own numbers... An honor code of sorts perhaps?"

The captain shrugged. "Space samurai." He said, simply.

"Something like that," The admiral agreed, "I've noticed that they behaved similarly on the ground; they didn't hesitate to kill, but they never out-numbered any of our people, though they could have easily." She stepped out onto the bridge, and several members of the crew turned in her direction, recognizing that she was about to give orders. The bridge was silent as The Admiral glanced over to the empty chair where the ship's communication officer had sat only a day earlier. He was the highest-ranking crew member to die at the first contact site, and the only death that had been visually recorded by the equipment that they had brought with them. She had watched him die nearly a hundred times over the last twelve hours. He had come to represent, in her mind, all of the 35 deaths and 15 injuries, most of which were only recorded by the biometric scanners.

She forced herself to be resolute as she turned to the engineering officer. "Set up a link of all of our scanners and systems, including external cameras and diagnostic systems directly to the computer on board the Mercury, and tell them to record everything." She ordered him. He immediately turned back to his console and began to work. She turned back to the captain and said, "Tell the Mercury and the Aurora that we are going to break formation, but that they are to stay on course for Earth, no matter what happens."

"Yes, Admiral." The Captain nodded and turned to leave. The Admiral grabbed his arm.

"Make sure they understand," She said, spitting the words out one at a time, "no matter what." Her look was fierce

He swallowed visibly and said, "Yes, Admiral." once more before she released him from her gaze.

"Finished, Admiral" She turned toward the voice. It was the engineering officer.

"Very good," She said without smiling, "faster than I expected." He was about to thank her, when she turned away, and stepped toward the navigation officer. "All stop," She ordered, "and turn us to face the approaching ships. Let me know if the Mercury or the Aurora alter course at all."

"Yes, Ma'am" said the young woman at the controls. She was a small woman, with square shoulders and a severe face. Her blonde hair was tied back into a simple ponytail but was otherwise unadorned. The woman reminded The Admiral of herself at that age. She felt sad for just a moment, then composed herself and looked up at the status screen.

It was just as she thought. When the ships caught up, one of them continued on a course to intercept the Europa, while the other two hung back to observe. Samurai... Indeed.

The Admiral stepped forward, so that she was just to the left of and behind the navigation officer. Unconsciously, she placed her hand on the woman's right shoulder and squeezed good naturedly. The officer turned to look up at the Admiral, her blond ponytail brushing the older woman's hand. "Ma'am?" she questioned.

"Transfer control of the ship to the manual override interface."

The woman pushed a series of buttons on her control panel before rising from her seat. She moved around to the front of the bridge, where she was joined by the Admiral. Together, they grabbed some straps from within recesses in the deck and lifted a panel out of the deck plating. Setting the panel aside, the two women looked at one another briefly before the officer returned to her station.

The Admiral turned and climbed down into the small, cramped pit, and sat herself down in the dusty seat. She listened to the soft mechanical purr as the controls around her automatically adjusted themselves to a comfortable position. Surrounding her, status screens and terminals gave her access to almost all of the Europa's systems. From this point, a solitary person could control the entire ship if they knew what they were doing. She grabbed on to the hand levers, which were beside her on either side, and placed her feet on the two petals before her. Gently, she wobbled each of the control sticks and alternatingly depressed each pedal. No one on board felt it, but the entire ship, and all its 125 remaining crew members, wobbled slightly in space. They wobbled in such a way that would have been nearly impossible for the computer navigation system to reproduce.

"Let's see if they understand," she whispered to herself. She watched the alien ship. For a long moment, it simply hung in space, then, tentatively, it wobbled in such a random way, that only a sentient, abstract being could be controlling it.

"Good." She said simply under her breath, and checked her displays to see that the Mercury and Aurora were still moving away at full speed. She called up an order that the hatch above her should be closed. This was completed with some hesitation, and the only light in the small shaft was the glow of each of the panels and screens, allowing The Admiral's flagship to become an extension of her own body and mind.

A knock came to the door of Kate Tria's quarters on the SCS Mercury. It was a frantic, urgent knock. Kate called out that the owner of the rapping knuckles should enter. Her first officer burst through the door.

"Captain Tria! There's been an accident in engine room four. The reactor is overloading."

"What's the danger of meltdown?" she asked, quickly alert.

"Certainly, within the hour if something is not done to contain it."

Without responding, Kate pulled the command console from its place in the wall beside her bunk. She first called up the ship diagnostic schematic. The commander was right; the reactor was in the process of overloading.

"Sit." she barked at the commander, who quickly, nervously sat on the nearest thing, which was luckily her chair. He hit the arm before he hit the seat, however, and while it looked painful, he accepted the injury stoically, and sat rigid on the seat cushion.

Kate glanced away from the screen with a raised eyebrow. "At ease, commander." She instructed. The man deflated into the chair.

"Sorry, Captain" he whispered meekly, but Kate was already back to the console. She punched up the comm and requested to speak with the Lead Engineer. As his face appeared on the screen, he looked as disheveled as she knew she did. He must also have been awakened, but she could tell from the background that he was not in his quarters.

"Report," she ordered hurriedly.

"Captain, I'm not really sure what caused it," he began in the casual, never truly at attention, manner that any technician-type officer seemed to have when addressing a superior, "The containment buffer around core A-3 has breached. We're trying to make adjustments, and solve the problem remotely, but we're not having much luck."

"Could you and your team address the problem better at the Core?"

"Of course," he said condescendingly, "but that part of the ship has been sealed off due to radiation and the chance of meltdown." He looked annoyed with the need to explain the issue to her.

Kate repressed the desire to reprimand him, there would be time for that later. "You and your team get into EVAC suits, to protect from the radiation, and get into that core. We have to do everything we can to keep the core from melting down." The Engineer looked worried. "If you don't think that you can do it..." she started.

"It's not that," he said, squirming a little, "It's just..." he left the thought unfinished. "I'll get right on it, Captain" he said at last. The connection was terminated from the other end.

Minutes passed. Kate and her first officer didn't look at each other. They sat in silence. Waiting.

Moments before, she had been harried and stressed. She had needed to act quickly and make a difficult choice: Send a small team into a dangerous situation to attempt the repair or take the chance that the explosion resulting from the meltdown would take the entire ship with it. She was starting to have doubts about her decision. She was tentatively deciding to rescind her order, when her screen flashed, and the Engineer's face, under an EVAC suit mask regarded her from within.

"We're headed in, Captain" he said, a slight waver in his voice. She noticed that she was glad that the man was scared. She didn't like him.

This immediately made her stomach turn. She felt that she might soon be ill. In all her years as an officer, she had never sent men into a situation which she knew to be likely deadly, but what choice did she have? The safety of the many is more important than the safety of the few. That's what she had been taught, but where to draw the line? If she knew the odds, it would be easier. If she knew for certain that she was choosing between the lives of these men or the lives of all the crew, including these men, the choice would be easy, even obvious. However, she only knew that there was a chance that the exploding engine would damage the rest of the ship. It could just blow itself harmlessly out of the side of the hull. The engine would be lost, but it already was anyway. Even if the engineers stopped the meltdown, the Mercury was still limping back to port on one engine.

"Captain?" She couldn't see the look on the engineer's face, but she guessed it was worried confusion. She had been staring at him while she struggled internally.

"Go ahead," She said. She couldn't see if the engineer looked disappointed, but she thought she heard a resigned sigh. He knew that the core could explode at any second. He knew that there was a reason that he and his team would have to move through the two bulk-head doors one at a time, like an air-lock: to protect the rest of the ship from the area that they were walking into.

Kate switched her display to view the ship diagnostic screen. She saw the dangerous engine core, outlined in red. She saw the first hatch of one of the bulk-heads open, then close. She watched as the second door repeated the process with about the same timing. The men were inside.

She felt herself grinding her teeth. She felt helpless. She felt like she should be doing something, like she should be the one risking her life in the core room. However, she knew nothing about the engines. She would be useless. For all his arrogance, the engineer was the right man for the job, and it was everyone else's job to wait for him and hope that he succeeded.

After a moment, she felt the entire ship jolt sharply, throwing her slightly into the air. Something stung her wrist as she fell from her bunk. She hit the floor and bounced off. She was floating. She realized, immediately, what had happened. The engine had gone and the ships acceleration stalled.

She floated for several moments that seemed like hours. Then, just as suddenly as the gravity had disappeared, it returned, though weaker. She hit the floor nose-first, and the wind was knocked from her chest. Slowly, she rolled herself over. Her first officer was on her bunk, sitting up, looking even more stunned than she felt.

"Commander." She said sharply from the floor. He turned and looked at her. Surprise registered on his face. Immediately he was on his feet and helping her to hers. Blood dripped from her face onto her nightshirt. She ignored it.

When she was again sitting on her bunk, and he was back in her chair, she asked "Casualties?", though she felt that she already knew the answer.

The commander pulled a small console from his pocket and tapped it several times. "Biometric scanners report some minor cuts and scrapes… One broken bone… Several nausea…" He paused here, not wanting to say what was next, knowing that he didn't need to, "No -- fatalities except --" he didn't finish.

except for the men you sent to die… she finished the sentence in her head. "Dismissed." She said simply.

Her first officer rose out of the chair, "Captain, I -"

"Dismissed, Commander." She cut him off sharply. With wounded feelings, he left.

When alone, Kate looked down at her hurt wrist. Her bracelet was damaged. The third silver chain, the one in the middle, was lying on the floor near her bed. It must have caught on the corner of her console as she fell. She touched her wrist with her other hand, and then began to rub it slightly. For several minutes, she sat like that. Completely numb. Then, she turned and lay back down, where she wept silently into her pillow. She hadn't cried since she was a little girl.

Her tear-ducts ached from use after so long with none. She didn't care. She welcomed the pain. She deserved it. That and so much more. She couldn't be a starship captain. She didn't have what it took. Everyone had been right, she couldn't cut it, not really, and it was just luck that had even gotten her this far.

"Tria?" mused the giant, lined face of the Secretary of Defense.

Chairman Lee was looking up at the screen in his office. Secretary Tomen was on the left half of the screen. His face took up his entire half of the picture; Lee hated it when people put their conferencing camera right on their desk. Director Feist was on the right half, and Lee could see the xenobiologist's full form, standing in a large, tidy office. The contrast was giving him a headache. He looked away, removing his glasses to rub his eyes.

"She has a very good record." The secretary continued, "Why shouldn't we trust her opinion. She's handled five first-contact missions. There have only been seven such missions in history. I daresay that she is the most experienced --"

"That doesn't matter!" The director cut in with his nasal, almost whiney voice. "All of our research shows that it is not possible for a sentient race to be completely non-negotiating. They must like or want something. Remember when we thought that we were going to have an interstellar war with The Garrison? They ended up being totally appeased with the establishment of a sodium trade."

"That just proves my point," the secretary's voice boomed, after he was sure that the director was finished, "Tria led that mission. She's the one who figured it out. If she doesn't see the same potential here, then I'm inclined to trust her."

A small icon blinked in the corner of Lee's screen. He studied it for a moment, then decided to interrupt the conversation. He could see from the man's expression, that the Director of Xenological Relations was about to accuse the Secretary of Defense of warmongering and didn't want the discussion to go in that direction.

"Gentlemen," he addressed them, "I am just now receiving a video feed from the Mercury. It is marked 'urgent'. Would you like to share it with me?"

Both men nodded. "Of course," they said, almost together.

"Good," Lee made a small, sad smile and pushed a button on his desk.

As the image came into focus from the static, Lee heard a stifled gurgle through the still-open audio link with his advisors. It was a sound like someone who is startled while sipping coffee.

Kate Tria floated in space, completely in control. She and the Menace circled each other, not sticking to any spatial plane in particular. She could tell that he was trying to maneuver his nose to face her port side. She let him. When he fired on her port weapons bay, she rolled to stern, taking the shot on the thicker hull of her underside.

She maneuvered the roll into a turn, and fired her aft missiles, aiming for his engines. The missiles struck true. The Menace ship was not slower than Kate, it took the blow without care. It was showing arrogance. Her first instinct was to think of this as a weakness. Quickly she remembered her experience. Strengths and weaknesses are not the same for every race. She was making the mistake of assuming some humanity on the part of the Menace. Quickly, she considered the possible outcomes of this battle. As she evaded another shot, and returned another glancing blow, she played out the long-term consequences of her actions, and the actions of the Menace. Just before the Menace fired again, she made her decision, and knew that it would be the most important thing that she had ever done. The Menace was dangerous. And the Sol Council needed to know that action was a necessity. They needed to be spurred.

As the Menace guns flared, she rotated to stern, taking the blow on one of her wings, completely shearing it away from the ship. It was dramatic, and she knew it, but it did not really disable her maneuverability outside of an atmosphere. The Menace knew that. The crew knew that. But, the billions of people who must now be watching on the surfaces of the human planets might not realize.

The Menace faltered. Hesitated. It knew that she could have moved away from that blast. She returned fire, but she purposely moved sluggishly, as if her control of the ship was dampened. On her monitor, she saw the Mercury begin to alter course. It was returning to help. No! she thought, You have to keep moving! I must finish this, now!

As the Menace turned about, and fired once more, she quickly rolled to expose the aft engine compartment. She moved her most vulnerable, yet easily guarded spot into the path of the Menace weapon. She knew the effect it would have on the ship. More importantly, she knew the effect it would have on her audience. Despite the cost, she knew she was making the right decision.

The explosion was bright and terrible. For a moment, there was a small sun where Kate Tria had been. The Menace was knocked back several decameters by the blast, and the fragments of the SCS Europa were hurled outward at great velocity. Some of them struck the Menace. Some of them were simply incinerated. Some of the fragments were hurled at great speed toward the thousand human worlds, carrying with them a sense of horror and atrocity, which humans hadn't known for many centuries, the necessary courage and hatred that they needed to survive. Some of the fragments spun out toward the Menace worlds, carrying with them a resounding and final shout of war.

The Demon Hunter

The architecture was like nothing PurpleWater had ever seen, despite his ten years with the Archaeologists' Guild, and these last three years working directly with Master Terix. From the beach, it looked like the entire building was made of mortar, which they all thought would be a simple matter to enter, despite seeing that the original entrance had been long-since buried, perhaps dozens of feet below the grass. A high window looked promising, and a team was assigned to start building a scaffolding up to it. It was PurpleWater himself who had noticed the cavern in the hillside and suggested that perhaps it might lead to another entrance.

PurpleWater looked back into the twilight darkness of the cavern entrance. HuntingMantis, another one of Master Terix's assistants, and the captain of one of the cargo ships, the *Shark*, stood at the entrance, his long, silvery hair glowing in the sunlight filtering in behind him, highlighting his silhouette. He, perhaps, saw PurpleWater looking back at him because he shifted his stance abruptly, the small sword at his belt picking up some of the sunlight, sending it into PurpleWater's eyes.

"This is foolish, PurpleWater," he began, "Why would there be an entrance into the tower through a hill that surely didn't even exist when the ancients lived here?"

"Master Terix asked us to take a look," PurpleWater shot back, "It can't hurt."

HuntingMantis' face was in shadow, but he could picture the look of pleased incredulity clearly enough. He'd seen it enough times. PurpleWater waited for the inevitable, smiling lecture about HuntingMantis' greater experience, and the number of ruins just like this he's already explored, but instead he said abruptly, "Make it quick, then!"

Feeling triumphant, PurpleWater turned back to the darkness of the cavern, though as his eyes adjusted, he saw that it was really more of a hallway, the construction was not Krell architecture, however. The walls seemed to be roughly hewn stone, with sawn timber for support. "Someone built this!" he called over his shoulder.

HuntingMantis' voice came back, clearly indifferent, "Probably some settlers, trying to reach the ruins themselves, but they would have had even more trouble with the iron-core walls than we're having up on the surface."

PurpleWater had to admit to himself, the stone and wood construction of the walls did seem a lot like several other expansion-era Colonial structures he'd seen, not nearly as unique or interesting as the style of the building above. He reached out to run a hand across one of the rough, timber beams. "Why would they make such a permanent structure, if it doesn't go anywhere?" He turned back to his companion in time to see him shrug slightly, and turn to look away, his sharp profile suddenly outlined in the light from outside, which was strangely red and dim.

That's when the ground dropped from below PurpleWater's feet and slammed him on his side against the hard-packed earth. The rumbling continued for several seconds, tumbling him about on the floor, and dumping dust and rubble down on his prone mass.

"Was that an earthquake?!" he called out when he felt safe lifting up his head, but HuntingMantis' form was no longer silhouetted in the cavern entrance. The sky outside was blood-red and getting dark quickly. He needed to get out of this passage before it collapsed.

As he slowly stood, and began stepping heavily toward the dimming light, he heard the faint voice. "It's me!" It was an odd dialect, and certainly not a voice he recognized. More dust fell from the ceiling, and PurpleWater quickly covered his face with the collar of his tunic.

"Is someone back there?" he called weakly into the darkness of the tunnel. Did one of the workers from above somehow fall in here during the quake?

"It's me!" the voice insisted, less faintly this time. PurpleWater glanced once more back to the red-lit entrance, HuntingMantis had not reappeared. "I'm coming!" he called back to the voice and stepped deeper into the darkness. The earth shook once more, and one of the squarish stones fell from the ceiling toward him. Before the stone struck him to the ground, he saw, in the gloom on the floor ahead, a glint of light, as if off of a small piece of jewelry. Then the darkness was complete.

"It's me! It's me!" the voice was insistent.

PurpleWater tried to speak, but nothing came out. His mouth was full of dust, and his head was throbbing. He smelled blood. His own, he guessed. He dragged one hand up to his hair, and it came away slick and warm.

"It's me!"

PurpleWater opened his eyes, but the darkness was absolute. The entrance to the tunnel must have collapsed, or maybe the floor he was on fell into a lower chamber.

"It's me!"

He was going to die. He was going to die in a hole on the other side of The Isles from his home in Windfall. He thought of his grandmother, dressed in her favorite apron, mixing him a flatcake with her own wrinkled, brown hands. He thought of his fiancé, working in her father's forge, her smooth, silver hair tied up, her strong, tan arms bared to the shoulder.

"It's me!"

PurpleWater had finally worked some saliva back into his mouth. He spit and coughed and spit again.

"It's Me!"

"Who?" he finally managed to ask. He meant it to be an annoyed shout, but it came out weak and strangled. "Who's there?"

"It's me, Saxidaliel!"

Saxidaliel? That didn't sound like someone on the expedition. He was sure he knew everyone. Was that a Shay name?

"It's me, Saxidaliel!"

"Got it," PurpleWater said, still weakly, "Where are you?" "Just here! Can't you see me?"

"It's pitch black. I can't even…" he struggled and coughed up more dust, "I can't even see myself."

"That explains it," the voice was a strange timbre, a bit tinny, a bit soft, but not strained. "Let me help."

At the last word, PurpleWater saw a faint glow appear in the darkness before him. It was a small ring, lit but not casting light. It was brightly polished silver with a design he'd never seen before: a small skull with wings that would wrap around one's finger, not quite touching at the back.

"Is that… Is that your ring?"

"You can see me now!" the voice was excited again. "Come this way!"

The ring floated in the darkness before him, with no context. Nothing else was visible in the darkness, but it seemed it must be resting on the floor only a few feet from his face. PurpleWater reached out but could not quite manage to touch the ring. Painfully, he dragged himself along the packed earth, toward the image.

Half a meter closer, he stopped and coughed to clear more dust, and felt a stabbing inside his chest. He must also have broken a rib when the ceiling collapsed. He suddenly felt lucky that he was not completely buried.

When he managed to pull himself across the floor another few inches, the ring was within reach. He grabbed at it, but found something else in its place, a collection of small hard, knobby tendrils. The ring shifted as he grabbed them.

"What is this?"

"It's me!"

"These are-" PurpleWater snatched his hand away. Bones! These were the bones of a hand, around and through the ring. He could see nothing of them, but now he could hear them shifting slightly as the ring rolled a few inches toward him. "Are you… dead?" He could hardly believe his own question.

"I'm not sure I can die. Certainly, I should have by now"

PurpleWater simply stared at the image of the ring before him, not sure what to think.

"Go ahead, the voice said. Pick me up. Put me on!"

"You're… You're the ring?"

"It's me, Saxidaliel!"

"How-"

"It's Me!"

Against his better judgment, PurpleWater reached out once more, and grasped the ring in his left hand. He watched, as if not in control, as the ring moved toward where he knew his right hand was, and he felt the cold silver slip over the third finger of that hand.

As it came to rest, he felt it snug to fit his finger perfectly, then a feeling which was simultaneously warm and chill

spread from his hand into his arm. "What-"

"Be patient. This takes a few moments."

PurpleWater lay still while the sensation spread up his arm, past his shoulder, and finally into his still aching head. He felt, nonsensically, as if light shone from his eyes, though he still could not see anything save the silver ring, his own finger not even blocking any part of the ring's intricate design.

It's me, Saxidaliel! It felt like his own thought, but it was in the strange voice. "You're in my head!"

I'm on your finger.

"I can hear you in my head." I can hear you in your head too.

Like this? PurpleWater thought carefully.

Like that. The voice sent back.

How is this possible?

It's me, Saxidaliel.

I got that. He tried to think sardonically but couldn't be sure it came across.

You can't see anything. The voice sent, matter-of-factly.

I told you that.

I can help.

How.

You have to let me.

This is all very strange.

Just give me your eyes.

My eyes?

Give me your eyes.

How?

Let them go, and I'll take them.

"I have gone completely mad." PurpleWater spoke aloud.

Possible, though it shouldn't stop you giving me your eyes.

He sighed. *I'll try.* PurpleWater closed his eyes and tried to pull himself away from them internally. After a moment, he felt his own control of his eyes slip away from him, and the warm chill of the ring intensified in his head.

Slowly, the scene around him began to clarify. He couldn't really see anything: It was all still darkness, but he could know, first, where the floor touched him, then where the walls sat, and the broken ceiling above him. The room was clear, and before him was a skeletonized body, clearly an Imperial, one of his countrymen. Though Colonials had a similar skeletal structure, the bones had been in this place for at least 400 years, judging from the degradation, and there were no Colonials in The Isles yet at that time.

What are you?

It's me, Saxidaliel!

What is a Saxidaliel?

There was a pause then, a deep pause, and PurpleWater saw new images superimposed over the room around him. A metal-walled cabin with strange glass beds, a pair of others who look upon him with respect and adoration, one was a woman, beautiful, with golden-brown skin like an Imperial, but soft features and dark hair which showed her to be a Colonial; the other was a race of man he didn't recognize, like a Draklander but featherless, with a blunted face, and slimy skin. Is that a Lith? PurpleWater had never seen a Lith.

The vision left him abruptly.

I was the captain of the Demon Hunters.

The Demon Hunters?

You are easily confused.

You were a person?

I am a person.

The world quaked around them then. Saxidaliel's presence flared up in his hand, and he felt himself pushed over in time to avoid a few more falling stones.

He was on his back, a bit further away from the bones, more dust settling on his face and tunic. He shook and coughed and thought, *Don't do that!*

I saved us from the rocks!

You made me feel like a puppet.

Sometimes we are all puppets.

"Hmph!"

We should leave this place. Saxidaliel said after a moment.

We're closed in.

Not anymore.

PurpleWater looked up. A faint, flickering light was trickling down to them as if from around several bends in a tunnel above. *How are you at climbing, little puppeteer?*

In the short time PurpleWater had been trapped underground, the sky had gone from red to black, though he could still see the faint glow of the sun, and now he could see the cause of the strange darkness, as well as the earthquakes. In the distance, upon the horizon, he could see the Lover's Heart, and it was aflame. The mountain, the only part of The Lover's Isle which was visible at this great distance, seemed so tiny. Its top was missing, as if it had been clipped with shears, and it was spouting great arcing lines of fire into the air. Fine black ash was falling from the ink-black sky, and it had already begun to pile in crevasses and up against trees and buildings where the wind swept it. Small swirls of the ash were starting and stopping frequently along the ridgeline, and periodically great boulders crashed to the ground or out in the ocean. Light was coming in frequent violet pulses, as lightning flashed in every direction.

PurpleWater stood in a wide, jagged breach in the wall of the ancient Krell building, where it must have split during one of the earthquakes, one hand on the exposed iron core of the wall, the other holding his pained ribs. The climb had been short, made faster, perhaps made possible, by assistance from the strange Saxidaliel, who had saved him from falling back into the cavern below on two occasions. The building itself, at least the part he had stepped through to reach this point, was curiously empty of ancient artifacts. There were a few rusted lumps, and some bits of rotted wooden furniture, but there didn't seem to be much else. It looked as though other explorers, or looters, had already found a way into this monolithic structure. Outside, the team's longest ladder had fallen on its side, none of the members of his team could be seen nearby.

The young archaeologist stepped forward, and looked down over the ledge toward the beach, one hand resting on one of the large mushroom statues, which dotted the ruins on this island. At the shore he saw the *Shark*; HuntingMantis was there directing the others in loading the small ship. Nearby, the ruined remains of the other two ships floated near a steaming boulder. Some locals, a few Colonials from the small village on the other side of the isle, stood on the shore, watching while the men took cargo up the ramp.

Carefully, PurpleWater picked his way down the slope, flattening himself against the ground each time it shook beneath him. He descended into the dense band of trees and shrubs which separated the beach from the hills, and at the bottom he found himself on a wide, flat slab of mortar. He hunkered down to touch the smooth, dusty surface.

Someone is nearby.

Where? PurpleWater scanned the trees around him, only darkness hung between the trunks. *I don't see anyone.*

You are blind. To your right, about 15 meters.

This way? This is just shrubbery.

Keep going.

PurpleWater pushed through the undergrowth, and abruptly found himself before another slab of mortar, this one leaned away from a large smooth-walled passage. Flickering light was visible from inside. Cautiously, he stepped through the opening, and into the hallway. This was clearly ancient Krell architecture. It must have opened up in one of the quakes.

Aren't you wary of such tunnels during an earthquake? Saxidaliel asked.

We got out of the last one.

It was only a few meters before the tunnel opened up into a large chamber. A few torches glowed inside, illuminating a vaulted chamber of impressive scale. The ceiling was a seamless glass dome, though completely covered with the loam of thousands of years. On the floor of the chamber, smooth stone paths crisscrossed among patches of earth. In the center stood a large statue of a male Krell warrior, two of its arms up, as if in triumph, holding swords of an ancient style PurpleWater recognized, the other two outstretched ahead, holding what looked like boxy handbows with no limbs or stirrups.

"PurpleWater, bring me another torch!" Master Terix's voice cut through the stillness of the chamber, his accent very thick, as it usually got when he was excited about a find. The small Lynx was crouching on the ground, partly hidden behind one leg of the statue, his tall, triangular ears laid back, his brow furrowed at the tablet in his hands.

He was alternatingly glancing up at the statue and back to his tablet. A small stick of charcoal in his hands was scratching furiously across the rough paper.

"Master Terix?" PurpleWater reached for one of the torches stabbed into the dirt nearby, and lifted it to see "What is this?" A distant crash sounded from the way he had come, and a few streams of dust shook from the statue.

Terix spoke in excited tones without looking up from what he was doing. "This may be the most important find in my career, perhaps in the entire history of the

Archaeologist's Guild." He licked his lips, and gave a quick glance at PurpleWater, his eyes shining, briefly, in the torchlight. "This is the most in-tact statue of a Krell we've ever found, and I think it answers several long-standing mysteries about the nature of..." he cut himself off and stared at his own illustration. "Are you bringing that torch over here, or gawking at me?"

"Oh! Sorry, Master Terix." PurpleWater took several long, quick steps over to his mentor, and held the torch to cast light on the tablet.

"Not down here!" Terix waved the torch away with one large, furred hand. "Up there."

The young man looked up at the statue, raising the torch again to get a better look at the detail.

The island is crumbling.

Right! PurpleWater shook himself internally and looked away from the statue with some effort. "Master Terix, we have to get off this island..."

The Lynx didn't move. "This may very well be the first depiction which actually shows that the Krell used the Fire

Gonnes."

"The Lover's Heart is erupting!"

The Lover's Heart? The voice of the ring seemed surprised.

"This may not prove that the Krell created the Fire Gonnes or the Spell Cannons, but it does show that they existed concurrently..."

There was something very important on that island. Saxidaliel's attention began to drift noticeably, and PurpleWater could see the beginning of the fog of images begin to drift before him.

Terix was still talking, his accent deepening further, "The presence of two of the artifacts in the possession of this figure may show that they were even more prevalent than we once believed…"

The fog in PurpleWater's head coalesced into a vision of the woman he had seen last time. She was older now, her hair longer, her face lined. She stood on the peak of a mountain, looking out over the bright sea. She turned to him and smiled warmly -

"Enough!" PurpleWater's voice came louder than he'd planned, and the vision disappeared as the shout echoed in the otherwise silent chamber. Terix really looked at him for the first time since he entered this place. Another crash sounded from outside, closer this time, and the air snapped as a crack appeared on one edge of the dome, looking like a bright, leafless sapling in the torchlight.

"Master Terix, it's not safe here." PurpleWater implored, "We must get down to the boat, and get off of this island."

The archaeologist blinked and turned back to his sketches for a moment. "Of course, you're right, young man. We'll go as soon as I finish this last sketch."

"We must go now, Master" PurpleWater reached out to take his mentor by the shoulder, and upon touching him, felt the ring flare up once more and some of its power flow out of him and into Terix.

"Yes," Terix said suddenly. "We should be away from here."

Once they were under way it was a short walk through the woods to the beach, through which Terix continued to expound on the significance of the find. Twice, he tried to turn around to get one more look at some part of the chamber or statue and was finally convinced not to return when a major quake brought down the building on top of the hill. The dust from the collapse rolled past them as they emerged onto the beach.

When the dust settled, PurpleWater saw that HuntingMantis and his crew were still loading the last of the cargo on the ship. The *Shark* was a small, squat, single-mast, cog, just barely safe on the open sea. Usually, it served them simply as a way to transport extra crates of artifacts, or unexpectedly large pieces. With the two larger holks destroyed, The *Shark* would have to carry them all, and their supplies.

Demon! the ring said insistently in his head.

What?

There is a demon ahead of you, we have to kill it!

I don't see a demon.

The other ships were less damaged than they had seemed from a distance, but they were broken up enough to mean great repairs would be needed before they could sail again, repairs that might take days or weeks. Along the surf's edge, a dozen bodies lay as if freshly pulled from the wreckage. Several men sat on the deck of the cog, nursing wicked looking wounds. PurpleWater looked around for the expedition's magical healer, Attendant De'Rayd, and found him among the dead. Nearby, the villagers from across the island sat huddled together on the sand, a child among them was weeping softly.

Find a weapon, find the demon, kill it!

I can't think with you shouting in my head like that.

"Master Terix!" one of the sailors had shouted, seeing them emerge from the trees as the dust settled around them. Several others had been watching the hill where the building they had been trying to access only a short time ago, had just fallen in on itself. They all turned then to see and a few cheered as Terix raised a hand to greet the crew.

That's him, that's the demon. He's right before you!

HuntingMantis had come quickly down the gangplank to meet the pair as they approached. "We thought you two were dead for sure," he smiled, his sharp, handsome features marred by soot and blood, though there were no obvious wounds on him. "We are just about to cast off; only two more crates left to load."

Get his sword from him, slash his throat!

That's not a demon, it's just HuntingMantis.

Demon!

"We should leave now," PurpleWater said, "It's too dangerous here. I'm glad you waited as long as you did for us, but we shouldn't delay further." He turned to one of the men still standing around, a Colonial, Gregory, maybe or Diggory? "Get those villagers on the ship and leave the rest of the crates."

HuntingMantis snagged the man's shoulder before he could move, "Hold there. This is my ship," he said smoothly, without losing his smile, "We need those crates, and we don't need those villagers." *Slay him!*

PurpleWater felt his fist ball up, not under his control, he felt the sudden urge to crouch and spring at HuntingMantis, to tear out his throat, to claim his life.

Stop it! he shouted at the ring in his head. You are not in control of me!

"We can't just leave them, HuntingMantis" he said when he had regained control of his impulses. Had it been minutes, or had it just felt like it?

"You mean Captain HuntingMantis, lest you forget" his smile was fading, though the smoothness to his voice remained as ever. "We don't have the space nor food to take additional passengers."

Demon! Demon! Demon! the ring seemed to be chanting, trying to take over his body again, PurpleWater felt his face twist with anger and concentration.

"Are you alright my boy?" Terix asked from his side.

It's me! Saxidaliel the Demon Hunter! I will slay this demon!

"Yes, PurpleWater, you don't look well," HuntingMantis put on a concerned face, and touched PurpleWater's shoulder, almost gently. "come up on to the ship if you like, and rest. Don't worry, I'm fully in control here."

"It's me!" PurpleWater said, not in his own voice. "It's me!" Without thinking, he raised his right hand up to meet HuntingMantis' own. When the ring touched his bronze flesh, there was a tiny flash of brilliant light, and the taller man drew his hand quickly away. In that instant, PurpleWater saw. He saw HuntingMantis as Saxidaliel saw him. A twisting mass of interconnected motives and motivations. He could see the emptiness of the man's heart, the impurity of his soul, the ugly bolus of his misspent intellect, and perverse desires. There was nothing to see, and everything to see simultaneously, the embodiment of the man's evil made clear as sunlight bursting from his wretched soul. The images repulsed him. He felt the bile rise in his throat, and then the warmth and coolness of Saxidaliel's power rise into his throat to meet it and shove it back down.

Slay the demon!

PurpleWater felt his face twist with anger and concentration. "You can't control me!" he said aloud.

I can!

Wide-eyed, HuntingMantis went for his sword. PurpleWater, half in control, spun awkwardly toward the nearby crewman, who was gawking at the exchange. He felt the ring try to reach out with both his hands but managed to hold one back. The other grabbed the hilt of the long knife at the man's belt, and yanked it free, bringing it up in time to parry HuntingMantis' opening strike.

PurpleWater struggled to regain control as he watched the sword in his own hand thrust twice at HuntingMantis, deflected both times by the man's skilled parries. He lost his feet next, as they corrected his stance. He felt less awkward, less off-balance, and he parried three rapid strikes from HuntingMantis, who looked genuinely surprised and, perhaps, a bit worried.

I'm in control! he screamed at the ring inside his head.

The demon must die! the ring shouted back.

PurpleWater completely lost control then, feeling once more like a puppet on strings, he watched, helplessly as he went through the motions of combat against

HuntingMantis. The sword in his hand burned hot, and he saw that it was glowing deeply with a purple energy, the color matching that of the lighting around the distant, erupting mountain. From the corner of his eye, he saw some of the other crewmen take hesitant steps toward the melee, hands on the hilts of their swords.

A furious exchange of blows resulted in a deep gash across HuntingMantis' chest, and his sword point down in the sand nearly 3 meters away. PurpleWater swept at the man's legs with the back of the knife, cutting into his shins, and dropping him to the ground. He raised the sword above his head and braced to plunge it downward.

No!

We must kill him.

We can't kill him. You cannot force me to do this.

It's me!

PurpleWater struggled to hold the sword high in the air, felt as though he was pushing it beyond the limits of his arms, the knife was surely soaring among the clouds. The ring was there, pushing down, as if another, larger hand was upon his, forcing him to act.

Time seemed to freeze around him as he looked down as HuntingMantis' face. The man was frightened for his life, and PurpleWater was the one with the blade.

"I am in control!" He pushed back against the ring, gathered its power from every corner of his body, and shoved it back against itself.

"Yes! Yes!" HuntingMantis shouted, raising his hands to his face, and suddenly sobbing. "You are in control!"

The knife plunged then, broken from Saxidaliel's grasp, and sunk to the hilt into the sand beside HuntingMantis' face. PurpleWater released it and stepped back, shaking off the last of the ring's power.

He took a deep breath and looked around. Everyone on the beach was staring at him, waiting. Master Terix stood with one hand outstretched, as if to plead with him. Some of them men had their swords bared, finally, though hesitation still held them expressionless. "Leave those crates!" he shouted to no one in particular, "And get those people on board, now." Knives were sheathed then, and the crew sprang to follow his orders.

Perhaps not every demon must be killed. the ring said, the manic notes gone from its voice.

I'm glad you can see it my way.

Another quake shook the island as the last of the villagers were ushered on board, leaving only PurpleWater on the beach with HuntingMantis, who had rolled over onto his hands and knees. He offered the man his hand, but he waved it away, pushing himself to his feet, and limping toward the gangplank.

PurpleWater followed slowly behind, and once on deck, pulled the plank up behind him as one of the crewmen threw off the mooring ropes, and another unfurled the sail. An ash filled wind picked up then, and took the small ship away from the island, and toward civilization.

Please leave a brief, honest review of this book on Amazon or Goodreads, or your preferred book review service. For a small press, a few reviews can help a lot with discovery.

Browse our titles, sign up for the newsletter and more:
manawaker.com

Purchase Manawaker books in print and digital formats in our online store:
payhip.com/manawaker

Subscribe to Manawaker Studio on our patreon:
patreon.com/manawaker

Find all these things and more from this taplink:

Ichabod Crane
and the
Magic Lamp
and Other Stories

CB Droege

Just outside the small town of Sleepy Hollow, retired Music Executive Ichabod Crane has been spending his days at the palatial estate of wealthy agri-business executive Baltus VanTassel, tutoring his daughter, Katerina, in digital music production. When a strange man claiming to be from the VanTassel's ancestral homeland tricks him into exploring an ancient crypt to find a fabulous magic ring, his only companion is the daemon who inhabits the brass flashlight the wizard sent him in with.

Peacemaker

and Other Stories

CB Droege

Ander is a prince, diplomat, and soldier in the clockwork army. Upon
returning to his home from a months-long diplomatic mission, he
learns that his father, the king, is dying. His sister is ill from grief, and
their older brother is mad with power and an intense hatred of the
kingdom's enemies, among whom may be a long lost family member.
Ander's journey to discover the truth takes him beyond the borders of
the kingdom, and his duty to his king.

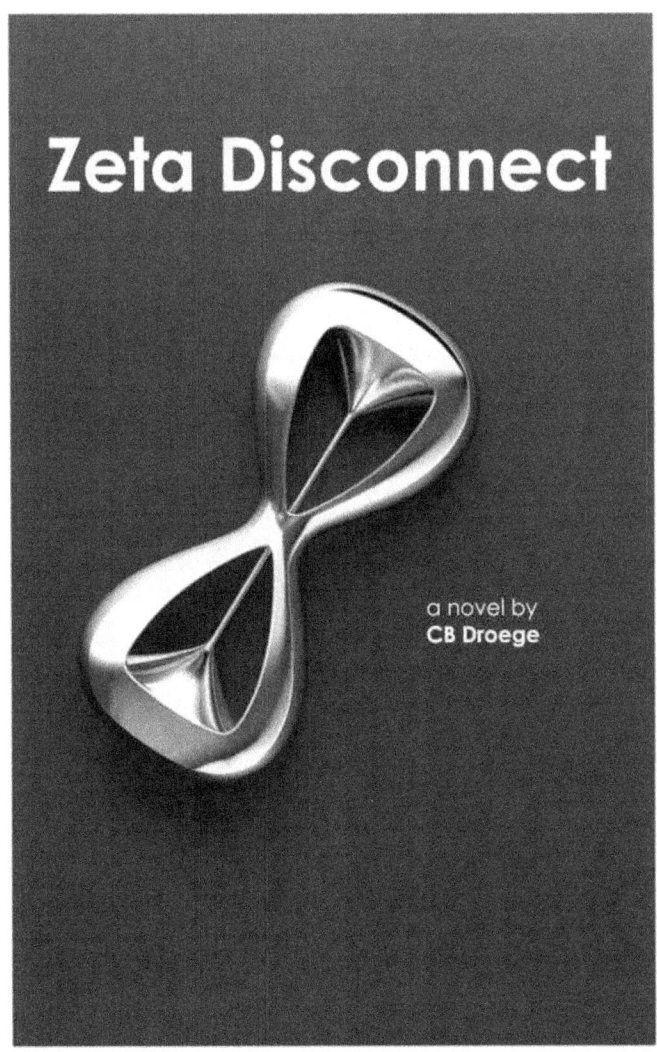

Zeta Disconnect

a novel by
CB Droege

Agent Z-4Q, of the Timeline Corrections Office has been sent into a broken, war-torn future on a seemingly routine mission. Each time he takes one of these missions, he is forced to forget everything about himself and his previous time with the organization, leaving him only with his training and the image of a pair of beautiful brown eyes, seared forever into his mind's eye. When he learns that he is the TCO's only remaining agent, and that the organization may not be working for the good of the people of the world, will he be able to subvert the organization's twisted agenda, or will they simply take his memories from him once more?

In this retelling of the Brother's Grimm tale The Sleeping Beauty, the administrator of the great Spincity Gamma Fald has invited twelve of the thirteen great A.I. scientists in his city to help him complete the programming for Briar Rose, the machine which will succeed him as Administrator. As each of these wise women work, they tell a story that exemplifies the gift they bestow upon the machine.

Rattus Futura

An Anthology of Future Rodents

Editor CB Droege

Rattus Futura is a collection of short stories, poems, and visual art depicting the various futures of humanity's ever-present stowaway.

Felis Futura

An Anthology of Future Cats

Editor CB Droege

Felis Futura is a collection of short stories, poems, and visual art depicting the various futures of humanity's most fickle companion.

DANGEROUS TO GO ALONE!

An Anthology of Gamer Poetry

WITH POETRY FROM
Glen Armstrong
Michelle Markey Butler
Kevin Cooley
Bryan D. Dietrich
Jacqueline DiOrio
CB Droege
Deborah Guzzi
A.J. Huffman
James Croal Jackson
Mathias Jansson
Sarah Frances Moran
Donald Raymond
Nick Romeo
April Salzano
Amanda Troutman
EDITOR
CB Droege

TAKE THIS. This brief collection of poems is about games. From D&D to *Half-Life 3*, many of us are shaped by the games we play. Some of those shapes are in this book.

Starward Tales is a collection of short stories, poems, and visual art retelling legends, myths, and fairy tales as science fiction.

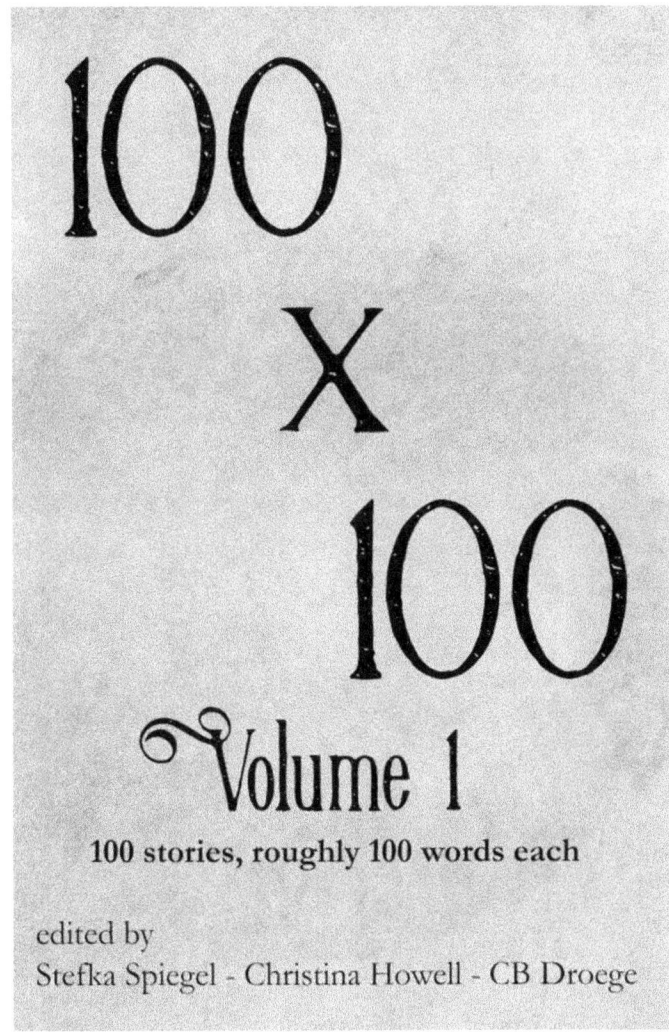

100
X
100

Volume 1

100 stories, roughly 100 words each

edited by
Stefka Spiegel - Christina Howell - CB Droege

100 word tales (or drabbles) are a storied and challenging form for writers of any genre. This volume collects 100 of the best stories from the first year of Creative Questers' 100wordproject, which encourages its members to write a new story each month on a specific theme.

Manawaker Studio's Flash Fiction Podcast features a new piece of short-short fiction each Thursday. The stories range widely in genre and theme, but lean a bit toward fantasy and science fiction. Hosted by CB Droege and supported by Manawaker's Patreon patrons

Find it on Spotify, iTunes, or wherever you usually get your podcasts.

From space cowboys to super heroes, from spy thrillers to young romances, *Quantum Age Adventures* tells stories from throughout Humanity's future. Joining you on this journey into tomorrow's past, a historian from the very distant future acts as your guide to this collection by providing explanatory notes which show how these very different stories tie into a larger narrative.

This book is the complete collection of the The Recycled Comics project, which used old abandoned comic book art, and gave it new life by writing a new story that tied the previously unconnected art together into an exciting and interesting sci-fi world.

The Book
of
The Isles
of the Sun
A nautical campaign setting

CB
Droege

The Isles of the Sun is a d20 campaign setting with a nautical flavor. The Isles feature a victorianesque imperial society on the brink of major change and potential upheaval. The book gives GMs and players everything they need to adventure in the isles, including new races, prestige classes, spells, magic items, feats, detailed information about Isles society, and hundreds of years of history. Mixed into the guide are tidbits of GMing wisdom from the author's over 20 years of GMing experience. Compatible with any d20 System rules set.

Dragon Line

A game for 2 players
by CB Droege
Second Edition

Incldes the expansion: Fade and Flow!

Dragon Line is a simultaneous-turns card battle with neat dragon art. The rules are very easy, and games go fast, but there is a lot of complexity to uncover, especially in understanding the ability combos.

Each player builds a small army of dragons with which to face their opponent, chooses in which order the dragons approach the enemy lines, and attempts to be the player with dragons remaining in hand at the end.

With clever drafting rules and thirty-five (now forty-nine) unique dragon cards, every hand of Dragon Line is a different game.

The Second Edition of Dragon Line has slightly updated rules, which reflect the data gathered from thousands of games played online over at boardgamearena.com (where anyone can try out the game for free). In addition, this edition contains the expansion "Fade and Flow".